THE STRANGE LOVE
of MARTHA IVERS

THE STRANGE LOVE
of MARTHA IVERS

MAPLE SPRING PUBLISHING

Published 2024 by Maple Spring Publishing

Front cover design by David Rheinhardt of Pyrographx
Interior design by Jason Snyder

Library of Congress Cataloging-in-Publication Data is available upon request

ISBN: 979-8-3505-0104-9

10 9 8 7 6 5 4 3 2 1

THE STRANGE LOVE
of MARTHA IVERS

Directed by LEWIS MILESTONE
Written by ROBERT ROSSEN
Based on *Love Lies Bleeding* by JOHN PATRICK
Produced by HAL B. WALLIS
Cinematography VICTOR MILNER
Edited by ARCHIE MARSHEK
Music by MIKLÓS RÓZSA
Production company: HAL WALLIS PRODUCTIONS
Distributed by PARAMOUNT PICTURES

CAST

Barbara Stanwyck . . . . Martha Ivers

Janis Wilson . . . . Young Martha Ivers

Van Heflin. . . . . Sam Masterson

Darryl Hickman . . . . Young Sam Masterson

Lizabeth Scott . . . . Antonia "Toni" Marachek

Kirk Douglas . . . . Walter O'Neil

Mickey Kuhn . . . . Young Walter O'Neil

Judith Anderson . . . . Mrs. Ivers

Roman Bohnen . . . . Mr. O'Neil

Ann Doran . . . . Bobbi St. John

Frank Orth . . . . Hotel Clerk

James Flavin . . . . Detective #1

Charles D. Brown . . . . Detective McCarthy

Blake Edwards . . . . Sailor (uncredited)

Robert Homans . . . . Gallagher (uncredited)

Gladden James . . . . John (uncredited)

T he camera shows the legend "Iverstown 1928" above a neon sign that says "E.P. Ivers."

It is night. YOUNG SAM MASTERSON is running down a street, past a POLICEMAN and a DETECTIVE.

Stopping in front of the door of a railcar, YOUNG SAM lets out a whistle. The door opens, and YOUNG MARTHA IVERS lets him in.

YOUNG SAM MASTERSON

Shut the door, quick.

The railcar is very dark. YOUNG SAM MASTERSON lights a candle. Thunder roars. YOUNG MARTHA IVERS runs into his arms.

YOUNG SAM MASTERSON

Scared of thunder?

YOUNG MARTHA IVERS

No, I like it.

YOUNG SAM MASTERSON

That's good, because there's going to be more of it. I brought you food, for the kitten too.

YOUNG MARTHA IVERS

Did you steal it?

YOUNG SAM MASTERSON

No, I bought it.

YOUNG MARTHA IVERS

Oh.

YOUNG SAM MASTERSON

And if we get caught, don't go making up any stories that I did. I'm in enough trouble as it is; you and your kitten.

YOUNG MARTHA IVERS

You want me to go back, Sam?

YOUNG SAM MASTERSON

Shut up.

YOUNG MARTHA IVERS

They looking for me?

YOUNG SAM MASTERSON

Your aunt's got every cop in Iverstown peeping through keyholes.

YOUNG MARTHA IVERS

You won't let them find me.

YOUNG SAM MASTERSON

You always come running to me.

YOUNG MARTHA IVERS

I've got nobody else to run to, Sam.

YOUNG SAM MASTERSON

The circus is leaving town tonight. Their train will go right through here. When it does, you just follow me. You run with all your might, and when you grab on, grab tight.

YOUNG MARTHA IVERS

Don't you worry about me, Sam.

The door rumbles.

YOUNG SAM MASTERSON

Hush, quiet.

YOUNG SAM blows out the candle. The door rumbles open, showing the POLICEMAN and the DETECTIVE.

DETECTIVE #1

There they are. All right, kids. Unless you got wings, you're caught.

YOUNG SAM MASTERSON

All right, Martha, let's go.

YOUNG SAM and YOUNG MARTHA descend from the train car, helped by the POLICEMAN and DETECTIVE. YOUNG SAM MASTERSON runs off.

YOUNG MARTHA IVERS

You'll never catch him; you'll never catch him.

Ignoring YOUNG SAM, the DETECTIVE and the POLICEMAN grab YOUNG MARTHA.

DETECTIVE # 1

Don't rough her, you chump. All right, miss, we'll take you on home to your aunt.

The scene changes to show MRS. IVERS in her study, writing. A knock on the door; it opens to show LYNCH, a butler dressed in white tie.

LYNCH

Mr. O'Neil to see you, ma'am.

MRS. IVERS

Show him in.

LYNCH

Mrs. Ivers will see you now.

MR. O'NEIL and YOUNG WALTER O'NEIL enter. They are both correctly dressed in suits and ties; YOUNG WALTER is wearing glasses.

MR. O'NEIL

Good evening, Mrs. Ivers.

MRS. IVERS

Good evening.

YOUNG WALTER O'NEIL

Good evening, Mrs. Ivers.

MR. O'NEIL

I have good news. Martha . . .

MRS. IVERS

What about her?

MR. O'NEIL

Martha has been found.

MRS. IVERS

I know.

MR. O'NEIL

Well, it was Walter who was really responsible for Martha being found. He told the police where she and that boy Sam Masterson usually go. Isn't that so, Walter?

YOUNG WALTER O'NEIL

Yes, Father.

MRS. IVERS

The boy will be rewarded.

MR. O'NEIL

Well, he's a good boy and he's bright. If I could afford it, I'd send him . . .

MRS. IVERS

Send him to a school like Harvard.

MR. O'NEIL

I guess I've mentioned it before.

MRS. IVERS

Many times.

MRS. IVERS rings a bell, and LYNCH enters.

LYNCH

Yes, madam.

MRS. IVERS

Take the boy to the kitchen, Lynch; give him some ice cream. You may give him a piece of cake too. Go along.

MR. O'NEIL

You must thank Ms. Ivers, boy.

YOUNG WALTER O'NEIL

Thank you, Ms. Ivers.

LYNCH leads YOUNG WALTER O'NEIL out.

MRS. IVERS

You've lost your pupil, Mr. O'Neil. I'm sending her away. I know why you offered to tutor Martha. I know why you've made Walter do his daily lessons with her. I know why you want him to live here. A scholarship for Walter, that's why. But I'm not a foundation, Mr. O'Neil. I don't care whether Walter drives a truck or goes to Harvard. Probably be a lot happier driving a truck.

Thunder rumbles. The scene is now the foyer to the house. LYNCH opens the front door and lets in the POLICEMAN, the DETECTIVE, and YOUNG MARTHA.

LYNCH

You are expected, Miss.

YOUNG MARTHA runs past him.

LYNCH

Oh, just a minute, Miss.

DETECTIVE #1

The name's Lundeen. You tell Mrs. Ivers the name of the detective who caught her is Lundeen.

LYNCH

I tell her.

LYNCH goes up to YOUNG MARTHA, who is holding her cat in her arms.

LYNCH

I'll take your furs, Miss.

YOUNG MARTHA IVERS

No.

LYNCH

You'd better, Miss; you know how she feels about that cat. I'll bring it up to your room. Your aunt is waiting for you.

YOUNG MARTHA opens the door to the study, slowly and cautiously, and enters. MRS. IVERS and MR. O'NEIL are standing in the middle of the room.

MRS. IVERS

Come closer, Martha.

YOUNG MARTHA advances a little.

MRS. IVERS

Closer, Martha.

YOUNG MARTHA goes up to MRS. IVERS.

MRS. IVERS

Look at me. You don't seem very sorry.

YOUNG MARTHA IVERS

I am. I'm sorry I was caught.

MRS. IVERS slaps YOUNG MARTHA in the face.

YOUNG MARTHA IVERS

No matter what you do, I won't cry.

MRS. IVERS

This is the fourth time you've tried to run away. Each time you were brought back here; no matter how far you got, you were brought back here.

YOUNG MARTHA IVERS

You don't own the whole world.

MRS. IVERS

Enough of it to make sure that you'll always be brought back here. Do you understand that? You understand that!

MR. O'NEIL

Your aunt doesn't deserve such an attitude, Martha. There not very many women who would be as patient and as kind, and there aren't very many little girls who would be as ungrateful.

MRS. IVERS

When will you understand that I'm doing all this for you, that I'm trying to wash the dirt and grime off you? Make an Ivers out of you again.

YOUNG MARTHA IVERS

My name is Smith, the same as my father's was.

MRS. IVERS

Your name is Ivers. I've had it changed legally.

YOUNG MARTHA IVERS

I don't care what you've done.

MRS. IVERS

Your name is Ivers: the same as your mother's was before she was stupid enough to marry that . . .

YOUNG MARTHA IVERS

Shut up, shut up.

MRS. IVERS

How dare you? You've still got his foul mouth.

YOUNG MARTHA IVERS

I won't let you talk that way about my father.

MRS. IVERS

Your father was a nobody, a mill hand. The best thing he ever did for you was to die.

YOUNG MARTHA lunges after MRS. IVERS.

YOUNG MARTHA

I'll kill you! I'll kill you!

MR. O'NEIL steps in to intervene.

YOUNG MARTHA IVERS

You get you off . . .

MR. O'NEIL

Martha, stop it.

MRS. IVERS

It's all right, Mr. O'Neil. Go up to your room and get into some dry clothes. After you've had dinner, I want to have a talk with you.

YOUNG MARTHA goes out into the hallway.

MR. O'NEIL

It's late out. I'll go get my son. Goodnight.

MRS. IVERS

Stay. I'm upset. I want someone to talk to.

MR. O'NEIL

Yes, Mrs. Ivers.

We now see the door of YOUNG MARTHA's bedroom open. YOUNG WALTER O'NEIL is there, holding the cat.

YOUNG WALTER O'NEIL

Lynch told me to sneak Bundles to you. I thought you'd be hungry. So I sneaked the milk too.

YOUNG MARTHA IVERS

She hates cats. She hates everything I like.

YOUNG WALTER O'NEIL

A policeman came to my house this morning. He asked me if I had any idea of where you could have gone. My father said it was my duty to tell them.

YOUNG MARTHA IVERS

Your father.

YOUNG WALTER O'NEIL

I didn't say a thing. No matter what my father told your aunt, I didn't say a thing.

YOUNG MARTHA IVERS

I'm cold; I've got to change my clothes. I'll leave the door open so I can hear you.

YOUNG WALTER O'NEIL

My father says you're foolish. My father says that someday you'll have everything in the world. My father says that if we only had one little part of what you'll have, I could go to Harvard.

MARTHA IVERS

You what?

YOUNG WALTER O'NEIL

I could go to Harvard.

Thunder rumbles, and the lights go out.

YOUNG MARTHA IVERS

The lights. What happened to the lights?

YOUNG WALTER O'NEIL

They went out. I think they went out all over the house.

YOUNG MARTHA IVERS

There's a candle and matches on the table, near the wall. Oh, you stand still. I'll do it.

YOUNG MARTHA lights a candle.

Back in the study, MRS. IVERS and MR. O'NEIL sit near the fireplace with a pair of lit candles. They are playing checkers.

MR. O'NEIL

Don't you think I'd better go up and see if Martha's all right?

MRS. IVERS

Martha will be all right, anywhere. Your play.

Back in YOUNG MARTHA's room, the thunder and lightning flash again.

YOUNG MARTHA IVERS

I am afraid of the thunder and lightning. Draw the curtains; I'm going to change.

YOUNG WALTER goes to draw the curtains; he sees the figure of YOUNG SAM, who raps on the window.

YOUNG WALTER O'NEIL

Martha.

YOUNG WALTER opens the window, and YOUNG SAM comes in.

YOUNG SAM MASTERSON

One peep out of you, and I'll break your nose.

YOUNG WALTER O'NEIL

I won't say anything, Martha. Martha will tell you I won't say anything.

YOUNG MARTHA IVERS

What? Sam! You see, Walter, I told you they'd never catch him.

She turns her back to him; her blouse is unbuttoned at the back.

YOUNG MARTHA IVERS

Sam, button me up.

YOUNG SAM buttons her blouse.

YOUNG SAM

I came to say goodbye. I thought it over, Martha; it's better for you here.

YOUNG MARTHA

I won't stay here. I hate her.

YOUNG SAM

All you have to do is play smart with her.

YOUNG MARTHA

I'm going with you.

YOUNG SAM

Now, you listen to me.

YOUNG MARTHA

I don't want to listen.

YOUNG SAM

It's late. I have to go.

YOUNG WALTER

Let him go, Martha. If he's caught here, he'll be sent to
reform school. Mrs. Ivers said so.

YOUNG SAM MASTERSON

They have to catch me first.

YOUNG MARTHA IVERS

All right, Sam, if you won't take me, I'll go without
you. I'll go off by myself.

YOUNG SAM MASTERSON

OK. Then let's go.

YOUNG MARTHA IVERS

I want to run up to the attic. I want to get a couple of
things.

YOUNG MARTHA goes out into the hallway, holding the candle.
We hear the meow of a cat.

YOUNG MARTHA IVERS

Sam, quick, Sam. Sam . . .

YOUNG SAM MASTERSON

What?

YOUNG MARTHA IVERS

She's going downstairs. Sam, my aunt!

YOUNG SAM MASTERSON

I'll get her.

YOUNG SAM runs down the stairs in the dark after the cat.

YOUNG SAM MASTERSON

Here, kitty, kitty.

YOUNG MARTHA IVERS

Have you got him? Have you got him, Sam? Hurry, Sam, the old witch will catch us.

MRS. IVERS goes up the stairs. The cat runs up the stairs behind her. Seeing the cat, she grows furious and starts walloping it with her cane. YOUNG O'NEIL and YOUNG MARTHA watch in horror, the scene lit by a candelabra that MARTHA is holding. YOUNG MARTHA goes down a few steps and hits MRS. IVERS with her own cane. MRS. IVERS falls all the way down the stairs.

The lights suddenly go back on, and MARTHA blows out the candles. MR. O'NEIL comes into the hallway and goes up to the fallen MRS. IVERS.

MR. O'NEIL

She's dead.

YOUNG MARTHA

We were upstairs. We heard a noise and we came down. We saw a man, a big man. He was leaving out of that front door. He left. See? It's open. And she was lying there.

YOUNG MARTHA holds out the cane.

YOUNG MARTHA

And this, this was lying there too. I picked it up. Isn't that true, Walter? Isn't it?

MR. O'NEIL

Is it, Walter?

YOUNG WALTER

Yes, father, it is.

MR. O'NEIL

Put it down. Put it exactly where you found it. Both of you better go upstairs. I'll phone the police.

YOUNG WALTER and YOUNG MARTHA are back in YOUNG MARTHA's room.

YOUNG WALTER O'NEIL

You will never get away with it, never.

YOUNG MARTHA IVERS

Your father believes me.

YOUNG WALTER O'NEIL

I don't know. I'm not sure.

YOUNG MARTHA IVERS

You keep your mouth shut.

YOUNG WALTER O'NEIL

But Sam, what about Sam? He was in the house. He saw it.

YOUNG MARTHA IVERS

Sam will never tell.

YOUNG WALTER O'NEIL

Yes, he will. He's scared. That's why he ran away after it happened.

YOUNG MARTHA IVERS

Sam won't ever tell.

YOUNG WALTER O'NEIL

Sam's scared; he ran away. I didn't. I stayed.

YOUNG MARTHA IVERS

No, no, he won't. Not Sam, not Sam.

MR. O'NEIL comes into the room.

MR. O'NEIL

I want to talk to you both. Sit down. Now, when the police come, you will tell them exactly what you told me. Do you understand, Martha?

YOUNG MARTHA IVERS

Yes, Mr. O'Neil.

MR. O'NEIL

And you too, Walter.

YOUNG WALTER O'NEIL

Yes, father.

MR. O'NEIL

You poor child. You'll be all alone in the world now, except for Walter and myself. But you needn't be afraid. We'll always be with you, Walter and I. We'll never leave you.

YOUNG MARTHA IVERS

Thank you, Mr. O'Neil.

The sound of a train signal. The scene shifts outdoors. It is very dark and raining heavily. A large train is passing. YOUNG SAM jumps onto a railcar, under a gaudily painted circus car. The train goes off.

The scene now shifts to IVERSTOWN, 1946.

It is night. A train is passing again. It goes past a railroad crossing at which a car is waiting. The train goes by, and the arm of the barrier goes up. The car drives through.

Inside the car, a radio broadcast is on. SAM MASTERSON is driving, with a SAILOR asleep in the passenger's seat.

RADIO ANNOUNCER

. . . Your competition at the fairground last week. In the handicap Chestnut King looks like an odds-on favorite.

SAM turns off the radio.

SAM MASTERSON

That guy doesn't know what he's talking about. Chestnut King's a dog. He was losing races to cow ponies years ago in Tijuana.

SAM looks ahead at a lit sign that says "Welcome to Iverstown." He turns to the sailor.

SAM MASTERSON

Oh, what do you know? What do you know about that? How do you like that, sailor? Leave a place when you're a kid, maybe 17, 18 years ago, and you forget all about it, and all of a sudden you're driving along and smacko! Your own hometown ups and hits you right in the face.

SAM looks at the road and realizes that he is headed straight for a lamppost, which the car hits. He gets out and opens the hood. The SAILOR is still in his seat, asleep.

SAM MASTERSON

End of the line, sailor. Come on, wake up.

SAILOR

Where are we?

SAM MASTERSON

In a small accident.

SAILOR

What happened?

SAM MASTERSON

The road curved, but I didn't. Come on, I've got to put into Iverstown for repairs.

The SAILOR ruefully gets out of the car.

SAILOR

Next time I'll pick me a guy that don't fall asleep.

SAM MASTERSON

Welcome to Iverstown. Well, maybe this time they mean it.

SAM MASTERSON's car pulls into a garage. DEMPSEY, the garage owner, is sitting, smoking, and reading a newspaper.

SAM MASTERSON

You got anybody here to fix this wreck, mister?

DEMPSEY

Roll her in.

The scene shifts to DICE GAMERS shooting craps in the garage.

DICE GAMERS

10 more, you don't make it. 5 more, you don't make it. Fat hot view, 2. Shoot.

Outside, SAM and DEMPSEY are examining the car.

SAM MASTERSON

How long will it take, pop?

DEMPSEY

Can't tell until we look her over. Come back tomorrow.

SAM MASTERSON

Open game?

DEMPSEY

Nope.

DICE GAMERS

Bet. Four. Right back, little Joe. A 1004. You got a bet? Come on, Harry. Make four. Seven, little Joe. Thanks. Shooting 20 and more. 10 ball, you don't make it than I do.

Back in the garage office:

SAM MASTERSON

What will it cost, pop?

DEMPSEY

Won't know until it's done.

SAM MASTERSON

Hey, now look, I want to know now.

DEMPSEY

Take it someplace else.

SAM MASTERSON

Welcome to Iverstown.

A radio broadcast begins.

RADIO ANNOUNCER

We interrupt this program of dinner music to bring you a special broadcast in the interest of the reelection of District Attorney Walter P. O'Neil.

SAM MASTERSON

Hey, no, leave that on, will you, sir.

RADIO ANNOUNCER

Ladies and gentlemen, it is with deep regret that we are forced to announce that Mr. O'Neil will not be able to address this citizen's forum tonight. Mr. O'Neil was suddenly taken ill. But we are fortunate to have the best-loved civic figure of Iverstown, the gracious Mrs. O'Neil, here in the studio tonight to speak for him.

MRS. O'NEIL

(on the radio) Citizens of Iverstown. The issues in this election are simple.

DEMPSEY

That's enough of that malarkey.

He turns the radio off.

SAM MASTERSON

This Walter P. O'Neil, isn't he the kid that used to live on Sycamore Street? His father used to be a schoolteacher.

DEMPSEY

Yeah, that's him. You know him?

SAM MASTERSON

Yeah. I used to; little scared kid on Sycamore Street. Now he's running for the district attorney. What's the odds?

DEMPSEY

On what?

SAM MASTERSON

The election.

DEMPSEY

No odds. No takers. This is a sure bet, mister. Going to be reelected, going to be governor, and I'm making book right now that someday he'll run for president. Yep. Going to be whatever his wife wants him to be.

SAM MASTERSON

Some gal. Who did he marry?

DEMPSEY

You from this town?

SAM MASTERSON

Used to be.

DEMPSEY

You ought to know her, then. Old lady Ivers' niece.

SAM MASTERSON

Martha Ivers?

DEMPSEY

Yep. Came into the whole works after the old lady died.

SAM MASTERSON

Well, what do you know? What do you know about that? Martha Ivers.

He goes over to a political poster that says, "Walter O'Neil for District Attorney." He looks up at a picture of the adult WAL-TER O'NEIL.

SAM MASTERSON

I don't know; you still look like a scared little kid to me.

SAM MASTERSON is now walking down a sidewalk, passing a storefront that says, "Tailor." He passes the POLICEMAN.

SAM MASTERSON

Hello, Gallagher!

POLICEMAN

Hey, wait a minute. Do I know you?

SAM MASTERSON

Sure. I'm the guy who tossed a rock through that window once. You're the guy who chased me.

GALLAGHER

If I chased you, I'll bet I caught you.

SAM MASTERSON

Come to think of it, I believe you did.

As SAM MASTERSON continues to walk along, he sees a house with a sign saying, "Rooms for Young Women."

TONI MARACHEK is walking out the front door. She is smoking a cigarette and carrying a suitcase. She sits down on the stoop. She sees SAM MASTERSON and crosses her legs enticingly.

SAM MASTERSON

Hello?

TONI MARACHEK

Hello.

SAM MASTERSON

You live here?

TONI MARACHEK

Used to.

SAM MASTERSON

Who runs this place?

TONI MARACHEK

A lady by the name of Mrs. Burke. She's not home.

SAM MASTERSON

You waiting for her?

TONI MARACHEK

Just came back to get my things. I've been away for a while. I'm waiting for a taxi.

SAM MASTERSON

I used to live here in this house 17, 18 years ago. I was born here.

TONI MARACHEK

Don't kid me, you're older than that.

SAM MASTERSON

Well, I didn't move right after I was born.

SAM MASTERSON sits down next to her and lights a cigarette.

TONI MARACHEK

Got one to spare?

He gives her a cigarette.

TONI MARACHEK

Got some more matches?

SAM MASTERSON

Here it is.

He lights her cigarette.

TONI MARACHEK

Got the time?

SAM MASTERSON

It's a quarter after 11.

TONI MARACHEK

I hate that. Just dandy. And I've got an 11:30 bus to catch.

SAM MASTERSON

You can still make it.

TONI MARACHEK

If the taxi doesn't show up fast . . .

SAM MASTERSON

You know anybody who lives around here by the name
of Masterson?

TONI MARACHEK

No.

SAM MASTERSON

Know anybody in town at all by that name?

TONI MARACHEK

No. I'm from Ridgeville. Is your name Masterson?

SAM MASTERSON

Yeah.

TONI MARACHEK

You mean you're just getting home after 18 years?

SAM MASTERSON

Well, 17 or 18.

TONI MARACHEK

You're just getting around to look up your people?

SAM MASTERSON

Well, not exactly. I just happened to be driving through
on my way west and more or less curious, that's all.
So good luck.

TONI MARACHEK

What you going to do?

SAM MASTERSON

What do you mean?

TONI MARACHEK

I mean about your people?

SAM MASTERSON

Well, I don't know. Maybe nothing. Maybe tomorrow I'll go down to the courthouse and look up the deaths in the last 18 years.

TONI MARACHEK

Can you do that?

SAM MASTERSON

Yeah, I think so. Good night.

He goes off. A taxi pulls up. TONI leans in and says to the driver:

TONI MARACHEK

The bus terminal. Please hurry. I've got an 11:30 bus to catch.

The taxi drives past and pulls up in front of SAM.

TONI MARACHEK

I thought it was you, Mr. Masterson.

SAM MASTERSON

I'm glad to see you again. I gave you my last match.

TONI MARACHEK

Want a lift to anyplace on the way to the bus station?

SAM MASTERSON

You talked me into it. You got my matches.

He gets into the taxi.

SAM MASTERSON

Got a name?

TONI MARACHEK

"Toni." Antonia. Antonia Marachek. Ain't that a dilly,
Mr. Masterson?

SAM MASTERSON

Sam.

TONI MARACHEK

Please hurry.

**The cab pulls up to a railroad crossing. The gate is down and
a train is passing through.**

TAXI DRIVER

The depot's just across the tracks. You still got four
minutes. You would've made it if you didn't stop to
pick up your gent.

SAM MASTERSON

You might be able to chase it.

TONI MARACHEK

I can get a bus back to Ridgeville tomorrow. Maybe I
won't get a bus back to Ridgeville. Maybe I'll go someplace else. Maybe in another direction. Chicago, fur-
ther west maybe. Have you ever been out west before?

SAM MASTERSON

Yeah.

TONI MARACHEK

I've never. Maybe I will. What's it like?

SAM MASTERSON

Big.

At the Iverstown bus terminal, a bus marked "Iverstown" pulls up. Another bus is just pulling out. The taxi pulls up, and SAM and TONI get out. TONI has missed her bus.

SAM MASTERSON

You want to go back?

TONI MARACHEK

I can't go back there. I have to go someplace else. Do you drink, Sam?

SAM MASTERSON

Yes, I drink.

TONI MARACHEK

I'll buy you one.

SAM MASTERSON

Okay.

A PORTER comes up to them.

PORTER

Too bad. Do you want me to check your bag in the station here?

TONI MARACHEK

I don't know. I guess I wanted a hotel.

SAM MASTERSON

You want me to take you there?

TONI MARACHEK

Do you happen to be at the Gable Hotel?

SAM MASTERSON

Yeah.

TONI MARACHEK

Can I go there?

SAM MASTERSON

It's a public place. Yeah. Tell the clerk that Sam Masterson wants a room for a young lady. She'll register when she gets there.

PORTER

Yes sir.

MASTERSON gives the PORTER a coin.

PORTER

Thanks!

MASTERSON and TONI walk into a bar past a neon sign that says, "Cocktails."

SAM MASTERSON

Classy. Blue lights, music, everything.

TONI MARACHEK

A cafe.

SAM MASTERSON

When I lived in this town, there were nothing but saloons. My father used to live in them.

TONI MARACHEK

Mine too.

SAM MASTERSON

We're related.

They sit down at a table. A WAITER comes up to them.

TONI MARACHEK

I'll have the same thing you have, if you don't mind?

SAM MASTERSON

Scotch. I take a plain water chaser with that if the Scotch isn't so good.

WAITER

Two water chasers.

TONI MARACHEK

Did you drive far?

SAM MASTERSON

About 600 miles since this morning.

TONI MARACHEK

You aren't driving anything tonight?

SAM MASTERSON

No, my Stanley Steamer's in the garage having her face lifted. *(to the waiter)* Better bring us a couple more before curfew.

TONI MARACHEK

Oh, that's fine.

WAITER

That'll be $2.

SAM MASTERSON

On me.

TONI MARACHEK

Oh, thanks. Maybe you'd like to drink to finding your people.

SAM MASTERSON

Oh, my mother wouldn't approve of that.

TONI MARACHEK

How would you know after all this time?

SAM MASTERSON

After all this time, you probably wouldn't care one way or the other.

TONI MARACHEK

You talk awful cold-blooded about them, don't you?

SAM MASTERSON

That's life.

TONI MARACHEK

Is it a big family?

SAM MASTERSON

No, it wasn't. Besides me, they're just the usual two people necessary to increase the population. Mother left when I was a baby, and my father probably drank himself to death by now.

TONI MARACHEK

Another man I know talks cold like that's my dad. He's the most cold-blooded man in Ridgeville. Once he kicked me. Gee, it made me sick.

SAM MASTERSON

I can guess why you didn't break your neck to catch that bus back to Ridgeville tonight.

TONI MARACHEK

I probably would've got on and got off before it started up. I would've got the jitters the minute I got on. Anyway, it's gone now for tonight, anyhow; there won't be another one until tomorrow night. And now I know for sure I'm not going to make that one either. Not the one to Ridgeville at least. But I'm so glad you came to have a drink with me tonight. I was so lonesome, I like to have died. Have you ever been that lonesome?

SAM MASTERSON

How lonesome is that?

TONI MARACHEK

About as much as you can hold without busting open. Want to know how I got that way?

The bar's lights start to flash.

SAM MASTERSON

Curfew. Shall we go home?

TONI MARACHEK

The reason I picked the hotel, your hotel, is really very . . .

SAM MASTERSON

You read the hotel advertising on that, when you had it.

TONI MARACHEK

You're smart. Maybe you think I've been trying too hard to get acquainted.

SAM MASTERSON

Maybe you have.

TONI MARACHEK

Maybe you think that's wrong.

SAM MASTERSON

Maybe it's too soon to tell.

TONI MARACHEK

I wonder what you're thinking.

SAM MASTERSON

I don't think you'll take up too much room in my Stanley Steamer.

TONI MARACHEK

Maybe you're all right.

SAM MASTERSON

You think you can hold that thought all the way to the coast?

They walk out of the bar. It is raining.

SAM MASTERSON

You'd better wait here for a minute.

They run under the awning of a furniture shop. The window displays a poster saying, "Re-elect Walter O'Neil."

SAN MASTERSON

I want to ask you something. Does that guy look like a scared little boy to you?

TONI MARACHEK

He looks like he's going to cry any minute. Let's get away from him.

The scene changes to the exterior of a stately house. A large, expensive car pulls up, and MARTHA gets out. A BUTLER comes to the door.

MRS. O'NEIL

Is Mr. O'Neil in?

BUTLER

No, madam. Not to my knowledge.

MARTHA goes in and climbs up a long flight of stairs. She goes into her bedroom. It is dark. She turns the light on. WALTER is asleep in bed, with his clothes on.

MARTHA O'NEIL

Walter?

WALTER O'NEIL

Hello?

He sits up. She does not reply.

WALTER O'NEIL

No words?

She lights a cigarette.

WALTER O'NEIL

Can I have a cigarette?

She hands him the cigarette that she has just lit.

WALTER O'NEIL

(taking the cigarette) My lady's lips.

MARTHA O'NEIL

I'll ring for some coffee for you.

WALTER O'NEIL

No, thank you. I'll have another drink.

MARTHA O'NEIL

Walter!

WALTER O'NEIL

If there's to be a discussion, I'll need another drink. Otherwise, I shall neither adhere nor be coherent when and if I reply to whatever it is you're about to say.

MARTHA O'NEIL

Did you forget that you were supposed to speak tonight?

WALTER O'NEIL

I didn't forget, I . . . It's nice, your room, I mean. It's been a long time since I've been here.

MARTHA O'NEIL

Where were you?

WALTER O'NEIL

Getting drunk.

MARTHA O'NEIL

Where?

WALTER O'NEIL

I'm still the people's choice. I did not make a public display of myself anywhere.

MARTHA O'NEIL

You realize, of course, that you will one day inevitably.

WALTER O'NEIL

Inevitably.

MARTHA O'NEIL

It's your career. Not mine.

WALTER O'NEIL

What's mine is yours.

MARTHA O'NEIL

Don't you think I'm entitled to an explanation?

WALTER O'NEIL

What do you want me to say?

MARTHA O'NEIL

I don't want to put words in your mouth.

WALTER O'NEIL

I'd prefer that you would.

MARTHA O'NEIL

All right. When did you get drunk? Where did you get drunk? Why did you get drunk?

WALTER O'NEIL

Don't stand over me like that. I'm a sentimental man, Martha. I started to get dressed, and then I realized it was the fourth anniversary of my father's death. I thought it'd be nice if I went to the cemetery and laid a wreath of flowers on his grave. However, I never got there. Sentiment overwhelmed me. I stopped off to have a drink to his sainted memory. As I drank, I thought to myself, it's such a pity that my father isn't alive, to be able to see for himself all his dreams come true. The dreams he worked so hard for. His son, a famous man, married to a beautiful and wealthy woman.

MARTHA O'NEIL

All right. Now tell me why you got drunk.

WALTER O'NEIL

Because I couldn't get up and speak before people.

MARTHA O'NEIL

Walter, listen to me, what's done is done.

WALTER O'NEIL

The deed's done, not the thought.

MARTHA O'NEIL

You've got a life to live.

WALTER O'NEIL

I don't know. I'm not sure.

MARTHA O'NEIL

A brilliant career.

WALTER O'NEIL

My father always said . . .

MARTHA O'NEIL

Your father was right.

WALTER O'NEIL

He was never right about anything. From the day he walked in and found your aunt on the floor.

MARTHA O'NEIL

I told you I never want that mentioned.

WALTER O'NEIL

The day he sat beside you in the courtroom as the public prosecutor demanded that the state take the life of a man for the brutal murder of Mrs. Ivers. My father said nothing. I looked at him, but he said nothing.

MARTHA O'NEIL

Your father was a realistic man.

WALTER O'NEIL

My father, may he rest in peace, was a greedy man.

MARTHA O'NEIL

The man they executed was a criminal. If he hadn't hanged for that, he would've hanged for something else.

WALTER O'NEIL

The man was a man. Justice is justice. That's the way it is. I can't get up and speak before people. The words stick in my throat. I had rather get drunk. I do get drunk. I did get drunk.

• 38 •

MARTHA O'NEIL

Walter, dear, listen to me. If you carry a thing in your mind, it makes you sick. I want you well. Tomorrow...

WALTER O'NEIL

It'll be like today.

MARTHA O'NEIL

You will leave on a trip for your health for a few weeks.

WALTER O'NEIL

Will you go with me?

MARTHA O'NEIL

No. I'll stay here.

WALTER O'NEIL

And I'll stay here too.

MARTHA O'NEIL

What do you want to do, give everything up? Is that what you want to do?

WALTER O'NEIL

You wouldn't let me do that, would you, Martha?

MARTHA O'NEIL

Do you want to?

WALTER O'NEIL

I don't know, Martha. I ask myself that question all the time. If my father were alive, I could ask him. Only I know what his answer would be. He'd say to me, keep what you have, and make her live up to it. Make her live up to her bargain. That's what he'd say.

MARTHA O'NEIL

I am living up to it, Walter.

He kisses her passionately. He picks up a liquor bottle on a table.

WALTER O'NEIL

There's another drink left, might as well have it.

He pours himself a drink.

WALTER O'NEIL

The bottle's empty now. Good night, Martha. Tell me, Martha, what should I do about my love? You tell me, Martha, why I don't abandon all this. Why don't I just throw it back in your face?

MARTHA O'NEIL

You tell me, Walter.

He leaves the room dejectedly.

SAM and TONI go up to the desk at the Gable Hotel. The CLERK is not in sight.

SAM MASTERSON

Now this is it. Not good, not bad.

HOTEL CLERK'S VOICE

With bath?

SAM MASTERSON

With bath, and come out, come out, wherever you are.

The HOTEL CLERK comes out.

HOTEL CLERK

With bath, hey. There are half as many beds as there are rooms. Half the rooms has baths and half hasn't. That's one way of looking at it. Another is for each two rooms, one has a bath in the middle and the other hasn't, or you might say there's a half a bath to each of two rooms.

SAM MASTERSON

How is that, again?

HOTEL CLERK

Now, there are half as many beds as there is rooms. And if the two . . .

SAM MASTERSON

Sorry.

HOTEL CLERK

I've already sent the boy with those bags up to your room, Mr. Masterson.

SAM MASTERSON

Oh, well, they belong to Miss Marachek here. They came in my name because she wasn't registered yet.

TONI MARACHEK

I missed my bus to Ridgeville.

HOTEL CLERK

Oh, that's too bad. The boy went off at 12. You'll have to manage yourselves. I can't leave the board.

SAM MASTERSON

Thanks.

The CLERK hands a key to SAM MASTERSON.

HOTEL CLERK

Good night. Sweet dreams.

SAM MASTERSON

Good night, cupid.

SAM and TONI go off. The CLERK looks at his hand. He hasn't gotten a tip.

SAM and TONI are in the hotel corridor.

SAM MASTERSON

25, your room number's 25. I'm 23. Makes us neighbors.

In the hotel room, the doors between their rooms through the bathroom are open. SAM goes into TONI's room and sets down her bags as she takes off her coat.

SAM MASTERSON

Why did you buy a ticket to Ridgeville if you didn't want to go back home?

TONI MARACHEK

I didn't. I didn't buy the ticket. I got it, but I didn't buy it.

SAM goes back toward his own room. TONI starts to sob.

SAM MASTERSON

You all right?

TONI MARACHEK

I'm a little cold, maybe.

SAM MASTERSON

You better get out of these wet clothes. I've started your bath for you. Hurry up now, I'm next.

SAM goes back into his room and closes the door.

TONI MARACHEK

Thanks.

We see TONI remove her dress. She is in her slip and has a huge smile on her face. We see her in the shower, with the same smile.

Then the scene changes to show TONI in her bathrobe after her shower. She is hanging up her dress. Then she knocks on SAM's door. He is lying fully dressed on his bed.

SAM MASTERSON

Okay?

TONI enters SAM's room.

TONI MARACHEK

I will loan you a book for a couple of cigarettes, if you don't mind what kind of a book it is.

SAM gets up and approaches TONI.

TONI MARACHEK

That pine soap makes you tingle all over.

SAM MASTERSON

That's something very personal about soap. It's almost as personal as a toothbrush.

TONI MARACHEK

I won't use your toothbrush.

• 43 •

SAM MASTERSON

Where's your book now?

TONI MARACHEK

You don't care what kind of a book it is?

SAM MASTERSON

Suspense is killing me.

TONI MARACHEK

It isn't my book. Somebody here before forgot and left it.

TONI holds up a Gideon Bible.

TONI MARACHEK

I warned you.

SAM MASTERSON

There's one in every room of the hotel. One in practically every room of every hotel in the world. It tells all about it there in the first page or so.

TONI MARACHEK

Well, what do you know?

TONI sits down on the bed and opens the Bible. She is about to get up.

SAM MASTERSON

Oh, no, no, no, don't get up. I want to look at you a minute.

SAM sits down in an armchair and looks at her admiringly.

SAM

That's really a picture.

TONI beams appreciatively.

TONI MARACHEK

Throw me a match. So you're leaving tomorrow?

SAM MASTERSON

Yeah, we're leaving tomorrow. That is, if the car is fixed.

TONI MARACHEK

Sure. You won't mind me being a passenger?

SAM MASTERSON

No, no. Glad of the company.

TONI MARACHEK

Are you going to stay in the west?

SAM MASTERSON

Maybe, maybe not. You might get lonesome again.

TONI MARACHEK

I've been lonesome before. I was so lonesome tonight. I like to have died.

SAM MASTERSON

I know you mentioned that.

TONI MARACHEK

But I tried to tell you why.

SAM MASTERSON

Look, I'm going to take a shower.

TONI MARACHEK

I just got out of jail. I just got out tonight.

SAM MASTERSON

Like I said, we leave tomorrow.

He opens up the Bible and sets it down on the bed next to her.

SAM MASTERSON

I think you'd like that.

TONI picks up the Bible and starts to read. He goes in to take a shower.

Then we see him come out after the shower, in his bathrobe. He sees TONI asleep on his bed. He looks at her tenderly, takes the Bible out from under her, and puts a cigarette in his mouth. Then he covers her with a blanket, takes a bottle of liquor, and goes into the other room.

The next morning, we see a newspaper shoved under SAM's hotel door. It has a huge headline, partly obscured by a sticker for the Gable Hotel, so that we read, "*DISTRICT ATTORNEY PROMISES UP VICE IN IVERSTOWN ON REELECTION.*"

Outside, we hear a DETECTIVE's voice:

DETECTIVE

Open up, sonny.

The key clicks in the lock and the door opens. A BELLHOP lets in two DETECTIVES.

We see two DETECTIVES in TONI's room. She is not there. It is dark. They go into the room where TONI fell asleep, but she is not there. One DETECTIVE picks up a piece of paper on the bureau and says to the other:

DETECTIVE

Try that door.

They go through the bathroom into Sam's room. The room is dark. SAM is sleeping. One DETECTIVE rolls up the shade, making a loud noise and waking up SAM MASTERSON, who jumps up, startled.

DETECTIVE #2

Good morning, Mr. Masterson.

SAM MASTERSON

You don't have to show me who you are. I can tell by the smell.

DETECTIVE #2

My nose isn't that big. I want to see. The chief sent us up here to ask you a couple of questions.

One of the DETECTIVES starts going through SAM's wallet.

DETECTIVE #3

Sergeant Masterson.

SAM MASTERSON

The suspense is killing me. What do you want to know?

DETECTIVE #3

You've been around. Look at that. Africa, Anzio, and Normandy. Why don't you wear that button in your coat?

SAM MASTERSON

The same reason you don't wear your badge. I like it incognito. Now what else do you want to know?

DETECTIVE #2

What we wanted to know, this layout told us. There ain't nothing you can add to it.

DETECTIVE #2 shows the note he found in the other room to SAM. The note says, *"Dear Sam, Gone to the bus station to cash in my ticket to Ridgeville —Back soon, Toni."*

SAM MASTERSON

She didn't get in an accident, did she?

DETECTIVE #2

She's in the can for a nice long stretch.

SAM MASTERSON

What's the charge?

DETECTIVE #2

Violation of probation.

SAM MASTERSON

Probation for what?

DETECTIVE #2

Theft. Terms of her probation when she was released yesterday was that she returned to her home in Ridgeville. An hour ago, we picked her up at the depot when she tried to cash the ticket.

SAM MASTERSON

Well, maybe she wanted to go by train. Maybe she wanted to walk. There's no law that says she . . .

DETECTIVE #2

That's not the reason she gave, wise guy.

SAM MASTERSON

No?

DETECTIVE #2

No. The reason she gave was that she'd got a job, said
you were her employer.

SAM MASTERSON

Well, what's wrong with that?

DETECTIVE #2

Nothing, if you can prove it. But take a tip from me,
bud. Don't try it. Jake and me don't like to waste our
time testifying in court, but we will. So long

DETECTIVE #2 picks up TONI's suitcase, and the two make
to leave.

DETECTIVE #2

Exhibit A, bud, in case you get stubborn.

SAM MASTERSON

Now wait a minute, copper. All right, leave her things
alone.

DETECTIVE #2

Do you want to come along, soldier?

The two DETECTIVES look at each other and leave.

SAM picks up the newspaper that had been shoved under
the door. He looks at a picture captioned, "Walter P. O'Neil,"
above a headline that says, "Prosecutor Promises Iverstown
Will Be Safe and Clean City."

SAM MASTERSON

A little scared boy.

SAM flings the paper aside.

SAM MASTERSON

You're just about to do your old pal a great big favor.

SAM MASTERSON enters the law offices of WALTER O'NEIL. He removes his hat for BOBBI ST. JOHN, the secretary who is typing at the desk.

SAM MASTERSON

How do you like the way the election's going this beautiful morning?

BOBBI ST. JOHN

The election's going good every morning.

SAM MASTERSON

Look, honey. Miss . . .

BOBBI ST. JOHN

St. John.

SAM MASTERSON

St. John.

BOBBI ST. JOHN

Bobbi.

SAM MASTERSON

Better still.

BOBBI ST. JOHN

What can I do for you?

SAM MASTERSON

In?

BOBBI ST. JOHN

In, but not yet ready to face the world. Won't you sit down?

SAM MASTERSON

Look honey, I'm in kind of a hurry here. Would you take a note in for me?

BOBBI ST. JOHN

When he buzzes.

She hands him a pencil.

BOBBI ST. JOHN

Here.

Inside WALTER's office, WALTER calls BOBBI on the intercom.

WALTER O'NEIL

I'll take calls now.

He goes to the liquor cabinet, pours himself a quick drink, and puts a breath mint in his mouth.

WALTER O'NEIL

Come in.

BOBBI comes in.

BOBBI ST. JOHN

There's a gentleman to see you. He says it's very important.

BOBBI hands WALTER a note. He glances over it.

WALTER O'NEIL

Tell him I don't want to . . . wait a minute. Never mind. I'll tell him myself.

WALTER braces himself, grins, and goes into the front office, where SAM is waiting.

WALTER O'NEIL

Sammy! Sammy Masterson!

SAM MASTERSON

Little Walter O'Neil.

WALTER O'NEIL

We were kids together, Miss St. John. I wouldn't have known you, Sam.

SAM MASTERSON

Oh, I wouldn't have known you either, Walter. Only I saw your picture.

WALTER O'NEIL

My picture. Oh, yes, yes, of course. *(turns to BOBBI)* I don't want to be disturbed unless it's very important.

BOBBI ST. JOHN

Yes. Mr. O'Neil.

WALTER and SAM go into WALTER's office.

WALTER O'NEIL

How long has it been?

SAM MASTERSON

Oh, 17, 18 years. Something like that.

WALTER O'NEIL

That long.

SAM MASTERSON

We were just kids. You remember, the three of us?

WALTER O'NEIL

Yeah, the three of us.

WALTER lights SAM's cigarette.

SAM MASTERSON

Thanks. What's she like, Walter?

WALTER O'NEIL

Beautiful. I married her.

SAM MASTERSON

I know, I know. You've done all right.

WALTER O'NEIL

I guess so. And you? What have you done?

SAM MASTERSON

Oh, knocked around. Seen a lot, I guess. You know, had some fun, maybe.

WALTER O'NEIL

What have you done mostly?

SAM MASTERSON

Lately or mostly?

WALTER O'NEIL

Mostly.

SAM MASTERSON

Gamble.

WALTER O'NEIL

You mean, gamble?

SAM MASTERSON

Sure, sure. That's my business.

WALTER O'NEIL

Perhaps this is where I should remark that all life is a gamble.

SAM MASTERSON

You don't need to bother. I know it. Some win, some don't.

WALTER O'NEIL

You needn't have made that point. Sorry, Sam. This has been a stuffy conversation. Oh, would you like a drink?

SAM MASTERSON

Isn't it a little early in the morning? I haven't even stopped for breakfast yet.

WALTER O'NEIL

The occasion.

SAM MASTERSON

You talked me into it. Fine, fine.

WALTER pours SAM a drink.

WALTER O'NEIL

Nice of you to look me up, Sam.

SAM MASTERSON

Well, I wouldn't have bothered you Walter, only I met a girl, and you can help.

WALTER O'NEIL

You don't look like you need help with any girl.

SAM MASTERSON

Well, this trip out, I do. This kid's in jail.

WALTER O'NEIL

What's the charge?

SAM MASTERSON

Violation of probation; name is Toni Marachek.

WALTER O'NEIL

That's not easy to square, Sam.

SAM MASTERSON

Oh, you can do it, and you will, for old time's sake.

SAM and WALTER raise their glasses.

WALTER O'NEIL

For old time's sake.

WALTER knocks back his whole drink at once.

WALTER O'NEIL

Thanks.

The intercom buzzes.

WALTER O'NEIL

Excuse me.

BOBBI ST. JOHN'S VOICE *(on the intercom)*

Mrs. O'Neil is here to see you.

WALTER O'NEIL

Please have her wait. She usually drops in on her way downtown.

SAM MASTERSON

Oh, I'd like to see her.

WALTER O'NEIL

(to the intercom) Have Mrs. O'Neil come in.

BOBBI ST. JOHN

Yes, sir.

MARTHA enters, sees SAM, and then halts.

MARTHA O'NEIL

Oh, I'm sorry. I didn't know you were busy. I'll wait.

SAM MASTERSON

Hello?

MARTHA O'NEIL

Hello.

SAM MASTERSON

My name is Masterson, Sam Masterson.

MARTHA O'NEIL

I'm sorry . . . Sammy Masterson!

MARTHA runs and gives SAM a hug.

MARTHA O'NEIL

Oh, hello!

SAM MASTERSON

Well, I'll do that again. Hello!

They hug again.

MARTHA O'NEIL

You should have called me.

SAM MASTERSON

I just came in.

MARTHA O'NEIL

Well, you've grown to be a big boy, Sam.

SAM MASTERSON

Well, I always was big for my age. You remember?

MARTHA O'NEIL

Yes, I remember.

SAM MASTERSON

Anything else you remember?

MARTHA O'NEIL

Oh, well, there are, there are lots of things.

SAM MASTERSON

I never figured that a skinny little mutt would grow up
so beautiful.

WALTER O'NEIL

I thank you for my wife.

SAM MASTERSON

It sounds funny.

WALTER O'NEIL

What does?

SAM MASTERSON

Well, your saying, "My wife."

WALTER O'NEIL

Does it?

SAM MASTERSON

Oh, so, don't get so, Walter. I mean, well, I've always thought of Martha as . . . Well, you know how it is. You keep something in your mind since the time you're a kid.

MARTHA O'NEIL

How long are you staying, Sam?

SAM MASTERSON

That all depends on our district attorney.

MARTHA O'NEIL

Oh.

SAM MASTERSON

Yeah. I may have to pull out in a couple of hours.

MARTHA O'NEIL

Oh, that's too bad.

SAM MASTERSON

That's the way things are.

The intercom rings again.

WALTER O'NEIL

(to the intercom) I don't want to be disturbed.

SAM MASTERSON

That's all right, Walter. You're a busy man, so I'll blow, and thanks. Thanks for everything. So long, Martha. Aren't you glad now you missed that circus train?

MARTHA IVERS

I don't know.

WALTER O'NEIL

Where can I reach you, Sam?

SAM MASTERSON

Oh, the Gable Hotel. And you will do that for me, won't you, Walter?

WALTER O'NEIL

I'll try my best.

SAM MASTERSON

You do that. And here's hoping you win that election.

WALTER O'NEIL

Thanks. I will.

SAM MASTERSON

What? Sure thing?

WALTER O'NEIL

Ask Martha.

MARTHA IVERS

Sure, sure thing.

SAM MASTERSON

What odds are you giving it?

MARTHA IVERS

Sure thing is never a gamble.

SAM MASTERSON

No. What odds will you give that that's a fact?

SAM leaves and closes the office door behind him.

WALTER O'NEIL

Breezy character, Sam.

MARTHA IVERS

Thank you.

WALTER O'NEIL

Very sure of himself.

MARTHA IVERS

He always was.

WALTER O'NEIL

This is the first time I've ever seen you off balance.

MARTHA IVERS

I wasn't aware of it.

WALTER O'NEIL

I was.

MARTHA IVERS

It came as a shock.

WALTER O'NEIL

Yes, it did to me too. "Sam will never tell," I'll never forget you saying that.

MARTHA IVERS

What makes you think he will?

WALTER O'NEIL

What makes you think he won't?

MARTHA IVERS

How long has he been here?

WALTER O'NEIL

He came in last night.

MARTHA IVERS

Did he tell you much about himself? Where he has been, what he's been doing?

WALTER O'NEIL

I thought you'd ask what he wanted.

MARTHA IVERS

What does he want?

WALTER O'NEIL

He's playing it smart.

MARTHA IVERS

Sam was always a smart boy.

WALTER O'NEIL

All he wanted was for me to get his girl out of jail.

MARTHA IVERS

His girl?

WALTER O'NEIL

That's what he said he wanted.

MARTHA IVERS

What do you think he wants?

WALTER O'NEIL

What he can get. He's a gambler, a sharp shooter, an angle boy. They come through my office by the hundreds. Couldn't you see blackmail in his eyes?

MARTHA IVERS

I haven't your experience with criminals.

WALTER O'NEIL

You will, when Sammy starts to shake you down.

MARTHA IVERS

Release the girl; maybe he'll just take off and leave.

WALTER O'NEIL

Leave? Do you think he'll leave a touch worth millions?

MARTHA IVERS

There's only one way you'll find out. Release the girl. (to the intercom) Goodbye, Miss St. John.

MARTHA leaves. WALTER goes to the intercom.

BOBBI ST. JOHN'S VOICE (*on the intercom*)

Yes, Mr. O'Neil.

WALTER O'NEIL

I want a routine check on a Samuel Masterson, non-resident, registered Gable Hotel. Miss St. John, close the door!

BOBBI comes into WALTER's office and closes the door.

WALTER O'NEIL

(to Bobbi) Stay here, please. *(into the phone)* I want a routine check of all garages. One of them has his car. Stay here, please. I want to check up on all local banks. Get that private detective McCarthy, and tell him to come right over.

The scene changes to the O'NEILS' house. MARTHA comes down to the stairs to find SAM in the library, perusing a book.

SAM MASTERSON

I thought I might improve my mind while I waited.

MARTHA looks at the book.

MARTHA IVERS

Boswell's Life of Johnson? Surely you didn't expect to wait that long.

SAM MASTERSON

I was just going to look at the pictures. I found your message when I got back to the hotel.

MARTHA IVERS

I asked you to phone.

SAM MASTERSON

I figured you wouldn't mind if I came in person.

MARTHA IVERS

I figured you would.

SAM MASTERSON

Why?

MARTHA IVERS

You impressed me this morning as a man who would bet on anything,

SAM MASTERSON

Almost anything, depending on the odds.

MARTHA IVERS

I bet you'd like to hear the story of my life.

SAM MASTERSON

What do you bet?

MARTHA IVERS

My story against yours?

SAM MASTERSON

You got a bet.

MARTHA IVERS

Well, let's see. You left here September 27, 1928. We'll start from there.

SAM MASTERSON

Exact date. How come that's so clear in your mind?

MARTHA IVERS

Why shouldn't it be?

SAM looks appreciatively around the room.

SAM MASTERSON

You know, I used to think this was the swellest spot in the world, but you've really made it just that.

MARTHA IVERS

It used to be so dark and ugly when she . . . I hate it. Come on, I'll show you what I've done with the rest of the house.

They get up and go to the library door.

SAM MASTERSON

Okay, fine. I haven't been on a rubberneck tour in years.

MARTHA IVERS

Soon after my aunt died, the executors of the estate wanted to close the house and send me to school, but Mr. O'Neil . . .

SAM MASTERSON

Mister! You're kind of formal about your husband, aren't you?

MARTHA IVERS

No. I was speaking about his father. Mr. O'Neil was my tutor. You remember him?

SAM MASTERSON

Oh, yeah.

MARTHA IVERS

After my aunt died, he and Walter lived here.

SAM MASTERSON

Hmm. That was cozy.

They walk down a corridor of the house.

MARTHA IVERS

This is Walter's room.

They go in.

SAM MASTERSON

Rich. Very rich. Well, you lived here all the time then, huh?

MARTHA IVERS

Except for the few years I went to college. Mr. O'Neil, Walter's father, thought it would be good for me to get away for a while.

SAM MASTERSON

Mr. O'Neil, Walter's father, he sort of took care of everything, didn't he?

MARTHA IVERS

Yes. Yes. He took care of everything.

SAM MASTERSON

You didn't like that?

MARTHA IVERS

Let's talk about something else.

SAM MASTERSON

What do you want to talk about?

MARTHA IVERS

Pick a subject.

They go into the dining room.

MARTHA IVERS

This is the dining room.

SAM MASTERSON

Isn't it kind of crowded? All right, I pick Walter as my subject. When did you marry him?

MARTHA IVERS

When or why?

SAM MASTERSON

I asked when.

MARTHA IVERS

When I finished school.

SAM MASTERSON

All right, now, why did you marry him?

MARTHA IVERS

Pick another subject.

SAM MASTERSON

It's your turn.

MARTHA IVERS

You.

SAM MASTERSON

An open book. I went out of this town with a circus. The one you were supposed to go with. Made friends with the animals and lived happily ever after, almost.

MARTHA IVERS

Almost?

SAM MASTERSON

I got ambitious in that tour, but good. It got so I wasn't satisfied just being friendly with the animals, I got so I wanted to own the animals. So I bought some animals. Well, my lion got the mange and gave it to the monkeys. The animals became a responsibility and a liability. I lost all my hard-earned cash and ran like a thief out of there with a great yen to become friendly with people. Now on that, I had some success. Me being a gambler and people being what they are. Well, that brings us up to my 21st year, when I became a man, officially.

MARTHA IVERS

How did it feel to become a man officially?

SAM MASTERSON

I felt I'd been there before. How did you feel about becoming a woman, officially?

MARTHA IVERS

I felt I'd been there too.

They go into MARTHA's old room.

SAM MASTERSON

Why, this is the room that you . . .

MARTHA IVERS

Do you remember, Sam?

SAM MASTERSON

Do I?

MARTHA IVERS

It's the only room I didn't change.

SAM MASTERSON

It seems that only yesterday I came through that window. We were going to run away together that night.

MARTHA IVERS

You do remember?

SAM MASTERSON

Yeah. And it was Walter who let me in.

MARTHA IVERS

I come here often, Sam.

SAM sits down at the window seat and picks up a doll.

SAM MASTERSON

Little girls grow up. They never get through playing with dolls.

MARTHA IVERS

There was a storm that night, thunder and lightning. I was afraid of the thunder.

SAM MASTERSON

Why, in the freight car that night, you told me you weren't.

MARTHA IVERS

I didn't want you to know. I wanted to be like you, never afraid of anything. You remember that too, don't you, Sam?

SAM MASTERSON

Things come back to you.

MARTHA IVERS

Don't say it like that, Sam, not to make me feel good, but because it's true.

SAM MASTERSON

All right, it's true. We were just a couple of kids.

MARTHA IVERS

We are not kids now.

SAM MASTERSON

No, Martha. We're not kids. No time for dreams.

MARTHA IVERS

Only one dream, Sam. And it came true. You're here.

SAM MASTERSON

So is Walter.

MARTHA IVERS

About Walter and myself . . .

SAM MASTERSON

Don't tell me.

MARTHA IVERS

I want you to understand.

SAM MASTERSON

I understand, Martha. I understood when I saw both of you together in the office. I watched the way he looked at you.

MARTHA IVERS

Sam, if you stay in Iverstown . . .

SAM MASTERSON

Well, I'm not staying in Iverstown.

MARTHA IVERS

I'm sorry, sorry that you ever left here.

MARTHA puts her arms around SAM'S neck.

MARTHA IVERS

Sam, for old time's sake?

SAM MASTERSON

Yeah. Sure. For old time's sake.

They kiss. Then SAM draws away slowly and goes to the door.

SAM MASTERSON

Bye. Martha.

The scene moves to DEMPSEY's garage. DEMPSEY goes into the garage office. The DETECTIVE, McCARTHY, follows him. The phone rings. DEMPSEY answers.

MR. DEMPSEY

Dempsey's garage. Oh yes, Mrs. O'Neil.

DETECTIVE McCARTHY

Mrs. Walter O'Neil?

MR. DEMPSEY

Yes, ma'am. Well, it was a rush job anyway, and I'm rushed enough as it is. Don't mention it. Glad to be of service, Mrs. O'Neil.

DEMPSEY hangs up the phone and addresses DETECTIVE McCARTHY:

DEMPSEY

You can add this to your report. Ms. O'Neil don't like this guy to go—not yet.

DETECTIVE McCARTHY

All right, Dempsey. Thanks.

We now go back to WALTER's office. DETECTIVE McCARTHY enters as WALTER pours himself a drink.

WALTER O'NEIL

Drink?

McCARTHY

Thanks.

WALTER gives him the drink, pours himself another, and drinks it down in one gulp.

DETECTIVE McCARTHY

There's not much to report on him locally. The out of town reports are still coming in. You'll have a complete file on him in a couple of hours.

WALTER O'NEIL

What's he look like so far?

DETECTIVE McCARTHY

Big-shot gambler, broke many times, but always turns up with a new bankroll. The police in every state have tried to find the source of his money, but no dice. Many arrests, no convictions; beat a murder rap in Frisco: self-defense; has a war record few can equal.

WALTER O'NEIL

The car in Dempsey's garage . . .

DETECTIVE McCARTHY

The ownership certificate says he owns it.

WALTER O'NEIL

What's wrong with it?

DETECTIVE McCARTHY

Smashed radiator.

WALTER O'NEIL

How long will it take to fix it? Well...?

DETECTIVE McCARTHY hands WALTER a note.

WALTER O'NEIL

Who did Dempsey get this call from? Didn't you check that?

DETECTIVE McCARTHY

Yes, I checked it.

WALTER O'NEIL

And who was it?

DETECTIVE McCARTHY

Mrs. O'Neil.

WALTER O'NEIL

That's all.

McCARTHY leaves. WALTER clicks on the intercom.

BOBBI ST. JOHN'S VOICE

Yes, Mr. O'Neil.

WALTER O'NEIL

Get me the county jail. I want the superintendent of the women's division.

The intercom clicks again, almost immediately.

WALTER O'NEIL

Yes?

BOBBI ST. JOHN

I have the county jail for you. Mr. O'Neil. Deputy Elizabeth Baker is on.

WALTER O'NEIL

Hello? That girl, the one I called you about before? Yes. Bring her out here at eight. I want to talk to her.

In front of the county jail entrance, it is night. SAM and another MAN are standing there.

MALE SPEAKER

You got the time, bud?

SAM MASTERSON

Yeah, it's five after eight.

MALE SPEAKER

Thanks. I'm expecting my friend out in a few minutes. Say, I ain't seen your face around here before?

SAM MASTERSON

No, I'm a stranger.

MALE SPEAKER

Then you ain't waiting for anybody, huh?

Oh, she's a stranger too.

MALE SPEAKER

Oh.

SAM MASTERSON

She was due out a couple of hours ago.

The two men continue their wait.

In WALTER's office, TONI is sitting in front of WALTER, who is at his desk. DETECTIVE McCARTHY is looking on.

WALTER O'NEIL

You are in a lot of trouble, Miss Marachek. The law is very specific on violation of probation.

TONI MARACHEK

It's specific about everything.

WALTER O'NEIL

You're serving a five-year sentence.

TONI MARACHEK

So I was told once before.

WALTER O'NEIL

You lied when you were picked up. You told the police you were employed by Sam Masterson.

TONI MARACHEK

You'd think they would've believed me if I had told the truth?

WALTER O'NEIL

Did he cook up that story between you?

TONI MARACHEK

He had nothing to do with it.

WALTER O'NEIL

You're very fond of him, aren't you? You wouldn't want anything to happen to him. Does he feel the same about you? You wouldn't want to serve out that five-year sentence, would you?

TONI MARACHEK

What are you getting at?

WALTER O'NEIL

Remember, five years, and this time you'll have to serve every day of it. You don't have to.

TONI MARACHEK

All right. Get down to it. What do I have to do?

WALTER moves away from her. TONI stands up. DETECTIVE McCARTHY approaches her to do the explaining.

In front of the county jail entrance, TONI is descending the steps.

SAM MASTERSON

Toni? Toni? Toni?

TONI almost walks past him. She stops and looks down on the ground.

TONI MARACHEK

Hello, Sam.

SAM MASTERSON

O'Neil phoned me, told me you'd be out at six.

TONI MARACHEK

O'Neil?

SAM MASTERSON

Yeah. Sure. The district attorney is an old friend of mine. I asked him to do me a favor and here you are. You're late, but free.

TONI MARACHEK

There was a mix-up; they lost some papers.

SAM MASTERSON

Oh, I got worried about you. What's the matter kid?

TONI walks along, staring uncomfortably at the ground.

SAM MASTERSON

Toni! Look at me!

TONI MARACHEK

I'd like a drink.

SAM MASTERSON

Ah, you're a cinch. I'll buy a dozen.

SAM waves to a taxi.

HEY, TAXI!

SAM MASTERSON

I'm going to toss you a real coming out party. Hey, taxi!

SAM and TONI enter an Italian restaurant. Then we see them seated. A WAITER sets a plate of spaghetti before TONI.

SAM MASTERSON

Spaghetti.

The WAITER sets another plate of spaghetti in front of SAM.

SAM MASTERSON

Hmm, that looks wonderful.

WAITER

I think you'll like it.

SAM digs into his dinner. TONI does not touch hers.

SAM MASTERSON

Go ahead, eat.

TONI MARACHEK

Guess I'm not hungry. My stomach's in a knot.

SAM passes TONI her glass of wine.

SAM MASTERSON

Here, this ought to help.

TONI MARACHEK

I'd have died if I had to stay on in jail.

SAM MASTERSON

Forget it; now you're out.

TONI MARACHEK

If you'd ever been in, you'd know what I mean.

SAM MASTERSON

I know what you mean.

TONI MARACHEK

A couple of times last night I tried to tell you why I did time; you wouldn't listen.

SAM MASTERSON

I don't want to now.

TONI MARACHEK

Oh, now you've got to, please?

SAM MASTERSON

All right, if it will make you feel any better.

TONI MARACHEK

I want to be sure you understand. One to five, they gave me; one to five years, that is.

SAM MASTERSON

That's a long jolt.

TONI MARACHEK

It's forever. I did three months before I came to trial.

SAM MASTERSON

It can happen to the best of people.

TONI MARACHEK

I'm not the best of people. I'm just Toni Marachek. "Where'd you get the fur coat, Toni?" the judge asked me. "I met a guy," I told him. "He said he was in love with me. He gave me the coat." "A likely story," he said. I said, "But it's true, every word of it. I tried to pawn it because I needed the money." "Where is the man?" he asked. "I don't know." I said. "He took a powder. He blew, he flew to the moon." "You don't fly, Toni," the judge says. The charge is theft; you do one to five."

SAM MASTERSON

Well, how come they gave you probation?

TONI MARACHEK

First offense. You know what probation is?

SAM MASTERSON

Yeah, sure. A knife sticking in your back.

TONI looks behind her uneasily.

SAM MASTERSON

Still looking out for the cops? Relax. Now you're free.

TONI MARACHEK

I don't feel so good.

SAM MASTERSON

You want me to take you back to the hotel?

TONI MARACHEK

Oh no, no. Please let me sit here a while.

SAM MASTERSON

Yeah.

JOE, a disreputable-looking man in a suit and smoking a cig-arette, approaches their table.

JOE *(to TONI)*

Get your coat on.

SAM MASTERSON

What's the gag?

JOE

Get your coat.

TONI MARACHEK

All right, Joe.

JOE

I was up to your hotel. Nice layout you got there. Double rooms, connecting doors, and tall glasses. What did this guy tell you he'd give you when he picked you up?

TONI MARACHEK

All right, Joe, there don't have to be any trouble, forget it.

JOE

She's my wife.

SAM MASTERSON

Brother, you can have her, in spades. Now, beat it. You, too.

JOE

I just want to make sure.

TONI MARACHEK

Joe, there don't have to be no trouble.

SAM MASTERSON

No, there don't have to be no trouble.

JOE

There's got to be. Certain wise guys have to be taught a lesson. Certain wise guys have to be . . .

SAM MASTERSON

Where do you want it, here or outside?

JOE

Outside will do me fine. There's an alley through the kitchen door.

TONI MARACHEK

Sam.

SAM MASTERSON

Shut up.

JOE *(to TONI)*

Stay here.

JOE leaves, gesturing to three men, who follow him out the door with SAM.

Back at the table, TONI collapses in sobs. DETECTIVE McCARTHY approaches her table and sits down.

DETECTIVE McCARTHY

OK, sister, you did a swell job. Now blow.

TONI MARACHEK

Yes, sir.

TONI picks up her coat and leaves dejectedly. She goes out and sees SAM across the street in a car, being beaten up by the MEN. The car pulls away.

We now see a wooden rail fence with a sign pointing to *"Sunny Grove, Midbury, Iverstown."* Then we see SAM gripping onto the rails of the fence, helping himself up painfully. He climbs over the fence. He has something in his mouth. He spits it out. He opens his hand and finds a badge that says, *"Private Detective."*

A bus is passing by, and SAM waves it down. He gets into the bus, looking very beat-up.

BUS DRIVER

What happened to you?

SAM MASTERSON

Not a thing. I'm just made up for Halloween.

We now go to the Iverstown bus stop. SAM and some other passengers come out. SAM puts his hand to his mouth in pain. He moves away from the bus. Then he spies TONI headed for the bus. He pulls aside so she does not see him.

As TONI is getting into the bus, SAM pull her aside and says to the driver:

SAM

Go ahead, bud, she'll catch the next one.

The bus drives off. SAM takes TONI aside into an alley.

SAM MASTERSON

Cut that; crying is not going to get you anywhere.

TONI MARACHEK

I'll stop.

SAM MASTERSON

I ought to beat it out of you.

TONI MARACHEK

I think maybe I got it coming.

SAM MASTERSON

Why, why, why?

TONI MARACHEK

Last night in the restaurant, I kept trying to tell.

SAM MASTERSON

Come on, get down to it.

TONI MARACHEK

Before they let me out, they took me to the DA's office.

SAM MASTERSON

O'Neil, his name's Walter O'Neil.

TONI MARACHEK

Yeah, that's right. That's his name.

SAM MASTERSON

All right. They took you to his office.

TONI MARACHEK

He asked me a lot of questions, mostly about you.

SAM MASTERSON

About me?

TONI MARACHEK

About you and me.

SAM MASTERSON

Huh?

TONI MARACHEK

He kept asking me if I knew why you came here. He asked me that a couple of times.

SAM MASTERSON

What else?

TONI MARACHEK

Oh, a lot of questions. I forget.

SAM MASTERSON

Remember.

TONI MARACHEK

My head's mixed up.

SAM MASTERSON

Well, the goons, the ones who worked me over?

TONI MARACHEK

They just wanted to scare you. O'Neil doesn't want you in town. They said if I didn't play with them, I'd go back to jail.

SAM MASTERSON

Who said that? O'Neil?

TONI MARACHEK

No, no, the other man, Mr. O'Neil wasn't there by then.

SAM MASTERSON

You're kidding.

TONI MARACHEK

They said they wouldn't hurt you.

SAM MASTERSON

Much.

TONI MARACHEK

No more parole, they said, if I went for it. I'd do the whole five, they said, if I didn't. I went for it. Go ahead and hit me, Sam. I've got it coming.

SAM MASTERSON

The only thing you got coming, kid, is a break. I'm going back to town.

TONI MARACHEK

They don't want you here, Sam. I don't know what it is. But they don't want you here.

SAM MASTERSON

Like it or not, they got me.

TONI MARACHEK

Next time it'll be worse.

SAM MASTERSON

Look, I don't like to get pushed around. I don't like people I like to be pushed around. I don't like anybody to get pushed around. Kid, I'll tell you what you do. You grab the next bus out, and I'll meet you, wherever you say.

TONI MARACHEK

I'll go back with you.

SAM MASTERSON

Good. I wanted you to say that.

They walk off into the night.

The next morning, at the O'NEILS' mansion, JOHN, the butler, goes to the front door and finds SAM, still disheveled, standing there.

JOHN

Just a moment, sir.

SAM grabs JOHN by the arm and twists it behind his back.

SAM MASTERSON
Take me to Mr. O'Neil and you won't get hurt.

SAM grabs JOHN by the arm and pushes him in front of him.

JOHN
Yes, Mr. Masterson. I hardly recognized you, sir.

They go into WALTER's study and find him there.

SAM MASTERSON
Tell your man to ask Martha to come down here.

WALTER O'NEIL
Tell Mrs. O'Neil that, John.

SAM MASTERSON
I thought we ought to have a little talk. Who'll kick off
first, your team or mine?

WALTER O'NEIL
You look terrible, Sam. Have a drink.

SAM MASTERSON
Thanks.

As SAM pours the drink, WALTER reaches into an open drawer
for a pistol. SAM slams the drawer shut on WALTER's hand
and punches him in the face. SAM collapses unconscious.
SAM puts the gun in his pocket, pours two drinks, and sees a
folder on the desk.

SAM MASTERSON
A report on Sam Masterson!

He drinks his drink and takes the other one over to WALTER,
who is slowly recovering consciousness.

SAM MASTERSON

Here, take this. I'm two up on you.

SAM hands WALTER the drink.

WALTER O'NEIL

Thanks.

SAM MASTERSON

You're out of shape. Walter. For a minute there, I
thought you were dead.

WALTER O'NEIL

I was—I wasn't going to shoot.

SAM MASTERSON

I wasn't going to wait and see. Come on. I took a gan-
der on this while you were out. I could have given you
a much more detailed picture on Sam Masterson. I
didn't know you cared.

WALTER O'NEIL

You know it now.

MARTHA enters in an elegant white, ankle-length coat.

SAM MASTERSON

Now I'll let Martha give it to you.

MARTHA IVERS

Give him what, Sam?

SAM MASTERSON

The facts concerning a guy called Sam Masterson and his attitudes towards life and love. Walter's got the wrong ideas.

MARTHA IVERS

Sam, you're hurt.

SAM MASTERSON

You ought to see the other guy.

MARTHA IVERS

What happened?

SAM MASTERSON

This.

SAM pulls out the Private Detective badge.

SAM MASTERSON

It fell out of a guy's pocket and hit me in the face. Private dicks. What's the trouble, Walter? Don't you trust your own cops?

WALTER O'NEIL

You're right, Sam. I hired the man who worked you over. The idea was mine. I thought it might scare you into not coming back. It hasn't. We're ready to listen to the current quotation on blackmail.

MARTHA IVERS

Walter!

SAM MASTERSON

Blackmail.

WALTER O'NEIL

I said blackmail. Now what is the price? Remember, you're dealing with two old friends.

SAM MASTERSON

Well, which one of you do I deal with?

MARTHA IVERS

With me. Be at my office at the plant at 3.

SAM MASTERSON

Okay.

SAM takes the drink from WALTER's hand, holds it up, and drinks it.

SAM MASTERSON

May the deal be profitable to all of us.

WALTER O'NEIL

Whatever the price is, that's it, Sam, don't try this again. What happened last night can happen again, and worse.

SAM MASTERSON

Don't try it, sweetheart.

SAM hands WALTER his own gun.

SAM MASTERSON

I'll make this a flat statement. I'll kill you.

The scene changes to a bathroom in the O'NEIL mansion.

MARTHA IVERS

Hold your hand under the water.

MARTHA helps WALTER wash his hurt hand.

MARTHA IVERS

Dry your hand. This will hurt.

MARTHA dabs iodine on the wound where SAM slammed the door on WALTER's hand.

WALTER O'NEIL

Even pain at your hands!

MARTHA IVERS

You were lucky.

WALTER O'NEIL

Yes. I'm a very lucky man.

MARTHA IVERS

And a stupid one. Yesterday afternoon, he told me he didn't want anything, but he was going away. Let me handle it.

WALTER O'NEIL

I didn't like what you had in mind. It's quite a thing in a small city like this to be a district attorney; you get to feel like God. You know everything down to the smallest detail. Even a call to Dempsey's garage. Sam's leaving Iverstown today.

MARTHA IVERS

That's what he said.

SAM MASTERSON

Want to hear you say it.

MARTHA IVERS

It's up to him.

WALTER O'NEIL

No, it's up to you. I know you, Martha. You are my life's work. I've studied you all these years. A little girl in a cage waiting for someone to let her out. And along comes Sam. Do you know what's on my mind, Martha, about Sam, I mean?

MARTHA IVERS

I think I do. And that's where it will stay: on your mind. Unless of course I tell you differently.

We are now at a lunch counter, where TONI is sitting. SAM sits down next to her.

TONI MARACHEK

What did O'Neil say? Do you think he'll make trouble?

SAM MASTERSON

No. No. I had him figured out, right? He's still just a scared little kid.

A WAITRESS approaches.

SAM MASTERSON

Coffee, please, black. No. Martha's the one I can't dope out.

TONI MARACHEK

Martha.

SAM MASTERSON

Mrs. O'Neil? The three of us grew up together. I told you about it, remember? *(to the WAITRESS, who sets down the coffee in front of him)* Thanks. She's beautiful. That's why I can't figure it out. Why should a beautiful, rich girl stay married to a guy she's not in love with?

TONI MARACHEK

How do you know that?

SAM MASTERSON

I know.

TONI MARACHEK

You sound like you're in love with her.

SAM MASTERSON

You sound like you're jealous.

TONI MARACHEK

Could be. When are we leaving?

SAM MASTERSON

This evening if the car's ready.

TONI MARACHEK

Well, what are we doing until then? I know. Why don't we find out what happened to your people?

SAM MASTERSON

Yeah. That ought to be simple. Now I know I left town September 27th, 1928.

TONI MARACHEK

It's the exact date. How come you remember it?

SAM MASTERSON

Wouldn't you remember a date, the exact date about something that happened that long ago?

TONI MARACHEK

No. Not unless something terrific happened that day.

SAM MASTERSON

Yeah. Come on, let's finish your coffee; we'll go down to the newspaper morgue.

TONI MARACHEK

The morgue?

SAM MASTERSON

Yeah. I think I can find out about my people down there. Afterwards, I'll take you shopping.

At the offices of the Iverstown Register, SAM is sitting at a desk. The IVERSTOWN REGISTER MAN brings over a large folio volume.

IVERSTOWN REGISTER

That was a strange case. It went unsolved for years. Then one day they picked up a guy who stuck up a garage or something. Someone who used to work at Old Lady Ivers' house. Came out at the trial and he was the one that knocked the old lady off. It's my favorite case. The picture of the guy.

SAM MASTERSON

Doesn't looked like very much, does he?

IVERSTOWN REGISTER

Yeah. Kind of a scared little rabbit. I watched him all through the trial. Never had a chance. O'Neil really did a job on him.

SAM MASTERSON

Is that Walter O'Neil?

IVERSTOWN REGISTRY

Yep. Same guy. It's kind of dramatic, though, him being engaged to the niece of the murdered woman. Sure did a job. Jury was unanimous.

SAM MASTERSON

What happened to him?

IVERSTOWN REGISTRY

Oh, they hung him. Interesting, eh? Solving a murder after all those years. It's all in the files there. Go ahead and read it.

SAM MASTERSON

Oh, thanks, I will.

MARTHA O'NEIL is in her office at the plant. The intercom rings.

MARTHA IVERS

Yes.

FEMALE VOICE

Mr. Masterson, by appointment.

MARTHA IVERS

Send him in, please.

SAM comes in.

SAM MASTERSON

Three o'clock, on the nose.

MARTHA IVERS

On the nose. Come in, Sam.

SAM MASTERSON

You should have kept me waiting. Big executives always keep people waiting. Didn't you know that?

MARTHA IVERS

Good executives don't.

SAM MASTERSON

I bet you're good.

MARTHA IVERS

I am.

They both look at a large, incomprehensible picture.

MARTHA IVERS

It catches it, doesn't it? The feeling of a factory?

SAM MASTERSON

When your aunt owned this place, I couldn't get past the gate; now I'm a guest, or am I?

MARTHA IVERS

I invited you here.

SAM MASTERSON

Martha, did your aunt leave you everything?

MARTHA IVERS

I was her only heir.

SAM MASTERSON

I'll never forget the way she looked that night, standing in the doorway, leaning on her cane.

MARTHA IVERS

I don't want to talk about it.

SAM MASTERSON

Okay. Okay.

MARTHA IVERS

You look different than you did this morning. Clean and fresh.

SAM MASTERSON

Yeah. Well, it's the perfume I use that makes me smell so nice. I bet I smell as nice as you and Walter put together.

MARTHA IVERS

What do you want?

SAM MASTERSON

I think I've got what I want. I think I've got a gimmick. A gimmick is an angle that works for you to keep you from working too hard for yourself. Simple.

MARTHA IVERS

Specifically, what is your angle?

SAM MASTERSON

Specifically, half.

MARTHA IVERS

Half of what?

SAM MASTERSON

You tell me.

MARTHA IVERS

All right, Sam, come here.

They go to the window and see a view of the mill and the town.

MARTHA IVERS

My father used to work here as a mill hand.

SAM MASTERSON

So did my father, when he was sober.

MARTHA IVERS

Now I own it.

SAM MASTERSON

Now you're even.

MARTHA IVERS

Now I'm even. I was 21 when I took it over. It had 3000 workers then, it's got 30,000 now. Ran as far as that gate. Now it goes down to the edge of the river. And I did it all by myself. Without Walter, without his father, all by myself.

SAM MASTERSON

Half of this should make quite a score.

MARTHA IVERS

Half would make you my partner.

SAM MASTERSON

That's what I had in mind.

MARTHA IVERS

You went out of here a dirty little kid once before; that can happen again. I don't have to give you anything if I don't want to.

SAM MASTERSON

But you do want to.

Back at the Gable Hotel, SAM rushes into his room.

SAM MASTERSON

Hey, Toni, come in here, quick.

TONI comes in the room from her own, wearing a sun suit.

TONI MARACHEK

Yes, Sam.

SAM MASTERSON

Make a wish.

TONI MARACHEK

I went shopping.

SAM grabs TONI in his arms.

SAM MASTERSON

Any wish. You make it, you got it.

TONI MARACHEK

You feel good?

SAM MASTERSON

Yeah. I'm high. I had a drink.

TONI MARACHEK

What was in it?

SAM MASTERSON

A bucket of gold. The dice came up 7. Toni, you bring me luck. I'm going to wear you like a charm.

TONI MARACHEK

You really think so, Sam; you really think I bring you luck?

SAM MASTERSON

I know so, and that's an asset for a guy in my business.

TONI MARACHEK

Toni Marachek, asset.

SAM MASTERSON

Toni Marachek, good kid. You stick around, Toni Marachek.

TONI MARACHEK

Now I've got all the luck. I'm funny that way. I say what's on my mind.

SAM MASTERSON

You walk down the street, and a girl asks you for a cigarette . . .

TONI MARACHEK

And a match and the time. Life is funny.

SAM MASTERSON

That's philosophy.

TONI MARACHEK

It's good too. You want to know how it is with me, Sam?

SAM MASTERSON

No. Tell me.

TONI MARACHEK

I've told you, and even if it's over, quick . . .

SAM MASTERSON

Look: what you don't know, don't talk about.

SAM and TONI kiss passionately.

TONI MARACHEK

I bought a new outfit; I want to show you.

SAM MASTERSON

Well, let's take a look at it.

TONI stands back so SAM can admire her sun suit.

TONI MARACHEK

$8.95. How do you like it?

TONI removes the skirt.

SAM MASTERSON

With you in it, it . . .

The door opens, and MARTHA comes in.

MARTHA IVERS

Hello, Sam.

SAM MASTERSON

Toni.

TONI MARACHEK

Yes, Sam.

MARTHA IVERS

I heard you talking.

SAM MASTERSON

Well, even a crummy hotel like this has a switchboard.

MARTHA IVERS

I have special privileges in this hotel, Sam. I own it.

SAM MASTERSON

It's Mrs. O'Neil, Toni.

MARTHA IVERS

Hello. So this is the girl?

TONI MARACHEK

Toni's my name, Antonia Marachek.

MARTHA IVERS

The sun suit looks very well on her. Sam, she's got just the figure for it. She's a very pretty girl.

TONI MARACHEK

I give another show at eight o'clock

MARTHA IVERS

In your room or here?

TONI is about to storm off.

SAM MASTERSON

Toni.

TONI MARACHEK

Yes.

SAM MASTERSON

Ms. O'Neil is sorry she said that.

TONI stops.

MARTHA IVERS

I'm sorry I said that.

TONI MARACHEK

Okay, forget it.

SAM MASTERSON

Toni.

TONI MARACHEK

Yes.

SAM MASTERSON

I'm going out with Ms. O'Neil on business. That's why
you came here, isn't it?

MARTHA IVERS

Yes.

SAM MASTERSON

I'll be back after a little while.

TONI MARACHEK

I've got no place to go. I'll be here.

TONI goes into her room and closes the door.

SAM MASTERSON

I didn't like that.

MARTHA IVERS

I apologized.

SAM MASTERSON

There was ice on your tongue.

MARTHA IVERS

If you want me to say anything else to her . . .

SAM MASTERSON

You spoke your piece. Let's get out of here.

MARTHA IVERS

I've never been in a hotel room like this before.

SAM MASTERSON

I've been in too many.

MARTHA IVERS

Just the way you read about it in books. Window shade. Scotch on the dresser. Let's stay here, Sam.

SAM MASTERSON

No.

MARTHA IVERS

Why not? We can order our dinner here.

SAM MASTERSON

I don't like room service.

MARTHA IVERS

All right, Sam.

SAM MASTERSON

Come on, let's go.

SAM and MARTHA are dancing together in a crowded nightclub.

MARTHA IVERS

What's your Toni Marachek really like?

SAM MASTERSON

That's what she asked me about you.

MARTHA IVERS

What are your plans for her?

SAM MASTERSON

Oh, she's very independent.

MARTHA IVERS

Hardly. How did you meet her?

SAM MASTERSON

We lived in the same house.

MARTHA IVERS

In Iverstown?

SAM MASTERSON

Yeah.

MARTHA IVERS

When?

SAM MASTERSON

Now . . . now and then.

The nightclub orchestra stops playing, and the audience applauds.

SAM MASTERSON

Well, let's go back to our drinks.

SAM and MARTHA go back to their table. The orchestra strikes up again.

MARTHA IVERS

To continue with your Antonia Marachek, have you other things in common?

SAM MASTERSON

Taxi cabs, hotels, and Bibles. And we don't like some of the same people and places.

MARTHA IVERS

All sounds like a very substantial beginning. How long have you known her, really?

SAM MASTERSON

Since the day before yesterday.

MARTHA IVERS

How long have you known me?

SAM MASTERSON

Martha, I'm not sure that I've ever known you. What do you say? Let's get down to business.

MARTHA IVERS

Let's get out of here.

SAM MASTERSON

Waiter?

WAITER

Yes, sir.

SAM MASTERSON

Check, please.

WAITER

Yes, sir.

At the bar, we see JOE.

JOE

Whiskey and soda.

SAM pays the WAITER.

BARTENDER

Thank you, sir.

SAM sees JOE.

SAM MASTERSON

Wait outside.

MARTHA IVERS

Sam, what is it?

SAM MASTERSON

Wait outside.

SAM steals upon JOE from behind, grabs him and punches him several times. He takes away JOE's gun.

WAITER

Beautiful, beautiful, beautiful.

SAM MASTERSON

Give that back to him when he sobers up. Tell him I run an honest book. I always pay off.

SAM and MARTHA are at the nightclub entrance.

SAM MASTERSON

I thought I told you to wait outside.

MARTHA IVERS

I wanted to see.

SAM MASTERSON

You saw.

MARTHA IVERS

You wanted to kill him, didn't you?

SAM MASTERSON

Yes, I did.

Now SAM is driving MARTHA in her convertible. She is wearing a kerchief over her head. They stop at a place that has a panoramic view of Iverstown.

SAM

That's the spot?

MARTHA IVERS

Yes.

SAM MASTERSON

I like your car. You know what happened to Lot's wife when she looked back, don't you?

MARTHA IVERS

What?

SAM MASTERSON

She was turned into a pillar of salt.

MARTHA IVERS

What happened to Lot?

SAM MASTERSON

Well, he got away. He didn't look back.

MARTHA IVERS

You know your Bible.

SAM MASTERSON

You would too, if you spent as much time as I did in hotel rooms.

MARTHA IVERS

I'll take it up. Come on, let's get out of here. I love to watch the city from this spot.

The two of them get out of the car.

SAM MASTERSON

From up here, it doesn't even look real, is it?

MARTHA IVERS

It's real, very real. Owning it gives you a sense of power. You'd know what I meant if you had it.

SAM MASTERSON

Ivers, Ivers, Ivers.

MARTHA IVERS

If anyone asked me my name now, I'd say it was Martha Smith.

SAM MASTERSON

I smell smoke.

SAM turns around.

SAM MASTERSON

Better take a look.

Behind them, we see smoke. SAM goes over and finds a fire burning. He tries to put it out.

SAM MASTERSON

Must have been some kids up here.

MARTHA IVERS

Sam, don't, let it burn. We used to come up here when we were kids and build a fire.

SAM MASTERSON

Ah.

MARTHA sits down by the fire and takes off the kerchief.

MARTHA IVERS

Let it burn, Sam. In those days, we used to think that this was real and that, that didn't even exist.

SAM MASTERSON

Just now you look like Martha Smith.

MARTHA IVERS

If only you hadn't run away.

SAM MASTERSON

Well, I waited for you. I remember I waited a long time in the rain, but you didn't show.

MARTHA IVERS

Give me a cigarette, Sam. If only you hadn't left town.
I had no one to turn to.

SAM leans over to light his cigarette from the fire and lets out
a garbled sound.

MARTHA

What did you say, Sam?

SAM MASTERSON

Nothing. I didn't say anything.

MARTHA IVERS

When I found out, it was too late. Much too late. One
thing led to another.

SAM MASTERSON

Another what?

MARTHA IVERS

I don't want to talk about it anymore.

SAM MASTERSON

No, go ahead, Martha. It'll do you good. Another what?

MARTHA IVERS

Where was I?

SAM MASTERSON

One thing led to another?

MARTHA IVERS

It would've been so different if you hadn't run away.
Would've been you instead of Walter, or if you had
stopped me when I lifted the cane . . . why didn't you
stop me? You knew how much I hated her. Why didn't
you stop me?

SAM MASTERSON

I wasn't there, Martha.

MARTHA IVERS

And then I stood there afterwards . . . you—you
weren't there?

SAM MASTERSON

No, Martha. I wasn't there. I left when your aunt came
into the hallway. I didn't want to stick around. I was in
enough trouble as it was. I never saw what happened. I
never knew until tonight about your aunt or that man,
the one they hung; a man that you and Walter killed.

MARTHA picks up a flaming stick from the fire and goes to
strike SAM, but he holds her off. He holds her arm behind her
back and starts kissing her passionately as she sobs. We see
her arm move to wrap around his shoulder as they both kiss.
SAM throws the flaming stick back into the fire.
   Later, the fire burns down into smoldering ashes.

MARTHA

[Crying] Sam, help me. Help me.

SAM MASTERSON

All right. Martha, tell me. Talk.

MARTHA

All right, Sam. I never imagined anyone could die so quickly. I'd always supposed that wherever I went, she would be with me. That she would never die. But it wasn't like that. I expected to find her when I went back to my room. Later I became frightened. The coroner and the police were sympathetic, the doctor very attentive. They believed my story, the one I told Walter's father. That night, I slept heavily, peacefully.

SAM MASTERSON

How did you sleep the night after they hung that man?

SAM MASTERSON

It wasn't long when I found out why Walter's father believed my story. It was as if my aunt had never died. He took her place. He wanted to make something of his son, and I was tied to them both from that time on. It became so unbearable that I wanted to tell the truth. But he had deliberately given me such a sense of guilt and had painted such a picture of what would happen to me that I was crazy with fear. He used that fear well. To increase it, he made me part of another crime. My testimony sent an innocent man to the gallows, and he used that to make me marry Walter. Sam, you're not going to go away again. I want you here, Sam. I've lived so much inside of myself, so choked off, wanting something else that lives and breathes, so desperate for air and room to breathe it in. Oh, Sam, please, please stay.

They kiss passionately.

MARTHA's car stops in front of the Gable Hotel. TONI is looking out the window. She sees SAM and MARTHA kiss.

SAM MASTERSON

Bye, Martha.

SAM gets out, and the car drives off. TONI looks distraught.
We see an ashtray filled with burnt cigarette stubs.
In the hotel, SAM knocks on TONI's door.

SAM MASTERSON

Toni, you still up? Toni?

TONI MARACHEK

Yes.

SAM MASTERSON

It's me. It's Sam. Can I come in?

TONI MARACHEK

Yes, Sam.

SAM MASTERSON

Mind if I put your light on?

TONI MARACHEK

In a little while. I was sound asleep, I've got a headache.

SAM MASTERSON

Okay. I've got something to tell you, Toni.

TONI MARACHEK

Yes, Sam.

SAM MASTERSON

Toni, you're crying. You're crying because you saw.
You were at the window there when we drove up. Well,
that's what I came in to tell you about, Toni: Martha
and me.

TONI MARACHEK

You didn't have to, Sam; no strings on this deal.

SAM MASTERSON

Well, that's why I wanted to. See, it started a long way back. I don't know yet how it's going to finish.

TONI MARACHEK

What do you want me to say?

SAM MASTERSON

I don't know.

TONI MARACHEK

What do you want me to do?

SAM MASTERSON

I don't know.

TONI MARACHEK

All you had to do is tell me the truth.

SAM MASTERSON

Like you did when those goons worked me over.

TONI MARACHEK

Now we are even: now I'm beat up.

SAM MASTERSON

I'm sorry I said that, Toni. Look, kid, I'm sore at myself, not at you.

TONI MARACHEK

Do you want me to leave?

SAM MASTERSON

Do you want to leave?

TONI MARACHEK

That's up to you, Sam. I'm here on a rain check.

SAM MASTERSON

Well, now don't put it that way. You're here because that's the way we wanted it.

TONI MARACHEK

And now?

SAM MASTERSON

I'm not sure. I'm just not sure.

SAM goes out of the room.

In the O'NEIL mansion, MARTHA enters the office. As she does, she hears WALTER on the phone.

WALTER O'NEIL

Hello, Gable Hotel? I want to speak to Sam Masterson.

MARTHA IVERS

Put that phone down.

WALTER O'NEIL

Hello, Sam. This is Walter. I know I'm not disturbing you. Martha just came in.

SAM MASTERSON (ON THE PHONE)

Well, what do you want?

WALTER O'NEIL

I want you to come up here, now, right now.

MARTHA IVERS

Are you crazy? The servants . . .

WALTER O'NEIL

I gave them the night off.

MARTHA IVERS

You're drunk.

WALTER O'NEIL

I had a lot to drink, but I'm not drunk. I suppose it would be stupid to ask where you were.

MARTHA IVERS

Yes, it would.

WALTER O'NEIL

Sam's not leaving, is he?

MARTHA IVERS

Ask him when he gets here.

WALTER O'NEIL

I just got my answer.

MARTHA IVERS

Then there are no more questions.

WALTER O'NEIL

No, I know what I need to know. Sam, the superman. Sam, the dirty little boy from the other side of the tracks.

MARTHA IVERS

I'll go and change. I wouldn't want him to see me in the same dress twice.

At the hotel, SAM knocks on TONI's door.

TONI MARACHEK

Come in.

SAM comes into TONI's room.

SAM MASTERSON

Toni.

SAM sees TONI putting on her coat.

SAM MASTERSON

You're leaving, huh?

TONI MARACHEK

There's a bus out in about an hour.

SAM MASTERSON

Toni.

TONI MARACHEK

Sam, it's, it's better this way.

SAM MASTERSON

Look . . .

TONI MARACHEK

Sam, I came back here with you because you said you didn't like to be pushed around. I liked you when you said that; you were looking for trouble, but it was a good kind of trouble. And now . . .

SAM MASTERSON

Now what?

TONI MARACHEK

Sam, I saw her. You're going to get hurt. Leave her, Sam, leave this town, even without me, but leave.

SAM MASTERSON

I can't, at least not just yet. You're going to need some money.

TONI MARACHEK

No, thanks. Let's break clean.

SAM MASTERSON

See you around.

TONI MARACHEK

Yeah. Around.

Back at the O'NEIL mansion, SAM is at the front door. WAL-TER answers.

SAM MASTERSON

Where's Martha?

WALTER O'NEIL

Upstairs, getting dressed for the occasion.

SAM MASTERSON

We'll go upstairs.

WALTER lets SAM in. They go upstairs.

SAM MASTERSON

Why did you call me?

WALTER O'NEIL

Got a riddle, Sam, maybe you can help me solve it. It's a little riddle called, "What's to be done about me, Martha, and you?" Sounds just like a poem. If it rhymed, it would rhyme with murder.

They go into MARTHA's room. She is there.

MARTHA IVERS

He's drunk. He's been sitting here drinking all night.

WALTER O'NEIL

Draw a chalk line and I'll walk it, or I'll take a mental test. Any question like . . . what is my object in life?

MARTHA IVERS

I tried to stop him from calling you.

WALTER O'NEIL

You're a wise egg, an angle boy. You know all the answers, don't you? How are you on dreams?

MARTHA IVERS

Then I was glad he called you. I was frightened of him, Sam.

WALTER O'NEIL

She was frightened of me! I had a dream, Sam. It was about you. In my dream, you were not a handsome corpse.

SAM MASTERSON

Maybe there was some other guy.

WALTER O'NEIL

In other dreams, there were.

MARTHA IVERS

I told you he's drunk.

SAM MASTERSON

Did you say others?

WALTER O'NEIL

Oh, little Martha. Life was so empty. Is that what she told you, Sam?

MARTHA IVERS

I don't want him in here, Sam. Make him get out.

WALTER O'NEIL

Now, you're all of them, Sam. Every one of them rolled into one.

MARTHA IVERS

Sam, make him . . .

SAM MASTERSON

Keep talking. I'm all of them rolled into one.

WALTER O'NEIL

Yes. You're a gymnasium instructor in Philadelphia with a muscle for a brain and a tendency to insipid verse. You're a guy, just a guy named Pete in Erie, who smells of fish and sings. You're last year's greatest fullback and you flunk your bar exam, but you wanted to be an industrial engineer. You're a guy who came along to fix a tire so well, you became a city paid inspector, and you're a lot of others, but worst of all, you're the one and only man who shares with me the only claim I have on her. Ask her, Sam, say to her, "Martha, is all this true?"

SAM MASTERSON

What if it is? What did you expect? She never wanted
to marry you. If you had any self-respect . . .

WALTER O'NEIL

She married me because she felt that way I would
never tell.

SAM MASTERSON

That's a lie. Your old man forced her. How long do you
expect her to go on paying off?

WALTER O'NEIL

Forever.

SAM MASTERSON

Whatever happens to you, you've got coming.

WALTER O'NEIL

What can happen, Sam? Shall I tell you? She'll try to
get you to kill me. Like she got me to send an innocent
man to the gallows.

MARTHA IVERS

I told you the way it was. It was his father's idea. He
made . . .

WALTER O'NEIL

Did she tell you how she stood up in the police station? How she looked at the man without batting an
eye? How she said, "Yes, that's the man. He's the one
who came into the house that night. He's the man who
killed my aunt." That even stuck in the throat of my
father. My poor, dear, departed, greedy father. But he
went right on, and so did I.

MARTHA IVERS

He's lying. You believe me, don't you, Sam?

WALTER O'NEIL

You believe her, Sam? Martha, at least tell the truth now. Tell how much you were afraid of an unsolved murder. Tell what a threat it was to the power and the riches that you'd learned to love so much—and that I'd learned to love too. Tell why I became district attorney. Tell why you made me hang that man. Tell the truth!

MARTHA IVERS

I told the truth. They were like leeches, both of them. They wanted everything.

WALTER O'NEIL

All I ever wanted was you.

MARTHA IVERS

Everything you want, everything you had I gave you.

WALTER O'NEIL

You gave me nothing.

MARTHA IVERS

Let that go.

WALTER O'NEIL

You're insane. You're out of your mind. Me too. You see, Sam, how close we really are to each other. Don't break up our happy home. It'll have to be you or me. And unless you do it now, it'll be you.

WALTER finishes his drink and walks unsteadily toward the door, clutching onto an armchair to keep from falling over.

WALTER O'NEIL

You mustn't think I'm drunk. I'm not. It's just that I'm
sick; inside of me, I'm sick.

WALTER goes to the doorway and has to steady himself on the
doorposts.

WALTER O'NEIL

Martha, help me, please.

WALTER walks out into the hallway. MARTHA puts her arms
around SAM.

MARTHA IVERS

Sam, you believe me, don't you?

They hear the sound of WALTER falling down the stairs. They
go out to find him unconscious and go down to examine him.
Halfway down the stairs, MARTHA clutches at SAM.

MARTHA IVERS

Now, Sam, do it now. Set me free. Set both of us free.
He fell down the stairs and fractured his skull. That's
how he died. Everybody knows what a heavy drinker
he was. Oh, Sam, it can be so easy.

SAM draws away from her and walks down the stairs to WAL-
TER. MARTHA looks on eagerly. SAM stands over WALTER.
We see MARTHA's face, with its look of cruel but triumphant
expectation. But this look turns to dismay.
SAM picks up the unconscious WALTER and carries him
onto a chaise longue in the office. MARTHA follows. She sees
SAM preparing a poultice for WALTER.

MARTHA IVERS

I thought you loved me.

SAM MASTERSON

I thought I did too.

MARTHA IVERS

Now you hate me.

SAM MASTERSON

Now I'm sorry for you.

MARTHA IVERS

And I dreamed about you coming back.

SAM MASTERSON

Your whole life has been a dream.

MARTHA IVERS

I thought you'd be the Sam I knew as a child.

SAM MASTERSON

Martha, you're sick.

MARTHA IVERS

I could run to you when I was in trouble.

SAM MASTERSON

In your mind, I mean, that's where you're sick.

MARTHA IVERS

And you'd help me.

SAM MASTERSON

So sick that you don't even know the difference between right and wrong anymore.

SAM pours a drink.

MARTHA IVERS

You've killed; it says so in your record.

SAM MASTERSON

I've never murdered.

SAM sees WALTER coming to. He gives him the drink.

SAM

Are you all right now?

WALTER O'NEIL

All right.

SAM MASTERSON

You fell down the stairs.

WALTER O'NEIL

I remember. You carried me in here?

SAM MASTERSON

Yeah.

WALTER O'NEIL

You had your chance, Sam.

MARTHA picks up the pistol from the drawer and holds it behind her back.

WALTER O'NEIL

It's a thin line, the one between life and death.

MARTHA IVERS

You said I didn't know the difference between right and wrong. What's right for Walter and myself—for us to tell the truth?

SAM MASTERSON

I think so. Yes.

MARTHA IVERS

And hang for it?

SAM MASTERSON

You wouldn't hang for it, not if you confessed; you'd do time, sure.

MARTHA IVERS

Sure, I'll rot in prison for the rest of my life. And for what? What am I guilty of?

SAM MASTERSON

Murder.

MARTHA IVERS

What were their lives compared to mine? What was she?

SAM MASTERSON

A human being?

MARTHA IVERS

A mean, vicious, hateful old woman who never did anything for anybody. Look what I've done with what she's left me. I've given to charity, built schools, hospitals, given thousands of people work. What was he?

SAM MASTERSON

Another human being . . .

MARTHA IVERS

A thief, a drunk, someone who would've died in the gutter, anyway. Neither one of them had any right to live.

SAM MASTERSON

You didn't think Walter had either. Bye, Martha.

SAM moves to leave, but MARTHA draws the gun on him.

MARTHA IVERS

Sam. Sam's going away. Did you hear what I said, Walter?

WALTER O'NEIL

Yes, I heard you.

MARTHA IVERS

We can't let him go, can we?

SAM MASTERSON

Martha's waiting for your answer, Walter.

MARTHA IVERS

We'd always be afraid of him. We couldn't live that way. We'd be fools to let him go, knowing so much about us.

SAM MASTERSON

You may have a little trouble squaring this one.

MARTHA IVERS

You broke into the house, you demanded money; you tried to attack me, and I shot you in self-defense. I have a right to kill in self-defense. That's what the law says, doesn't it, Walter? Isn't that what the law says, Walter?

WALTER smiles gleefully.

SAM MASTERSON

It'll hold up, Walter. A man with a police record. It's a
perfect case, if you can get Walter to be your witness.
Do you want to bet?

**Turning his back on them, SAM walks toward the door. MAR-
THA points the gun at him.**

SAM MASTERSON

I feel sorry for you, both of you.

**SAM walks out. MARTHA lowers the gun. MARTHA rushes to
the window to watch him go.**

WALTER O'NEIL

You love him.

MARTHA IVERS

I hate him.

WALTER O'NEIL

That's why you dropped the gun.

MARTHA IVERS

I was afraid. For the first time in my life I was afraid.
I felt you'd no longer stand by me. That you'd leave me.

WALTER O'NEIL

No, Martha, I believe you. I love you. Don't cry, Martha. It's not your fault.

MARTHA IVERS

It isn't, is it, Walter?

WALTER O'NEIL

No, nor mine. Not my father's, not your auntie's.

MARTHA IVERS

It's not anyone's fault.

WALTER O'NEIL

It's just the way things are. It's what people want and how hard they want it; how hard it is for them to get it.

MARTHA IVERS

He's near the gate. I'm glad he's going.

WALTER O'NEIL

He'll always be . . .

MARTHA IVERS

No, he won't, Walter, he won't. And he'll never tell. You needn't be afraid, and you'll see: things will be different now between you and me. Just like . . . just like nothing ever happened.

WALTER O'NEIL

Just like nothing ever happened. Will you kiss me, Martha?

They kiss.

MARTHA IVERS

You believe me?

We see WALTER draw the gun out of his pocket. MARTHA sees him and puts her hand on the gun, startling WALTER. MARTHA's hand pulls it toward her, and she fires it.

SAM'S VOICE (*in her head*)

Ivers, Ivers, Ivers.

MARTHA IVERS

No, Martha Smith.

She falls to the ground dead.

Outside, SAM hears the gunshot and runs back toward the house. He sees WALTER at the window, holding MARTHA's dead body. Seeing this, SAM walks away.

Back in his hotel room, SAM starts packing. The door opens, and he sees TONI.

TONI MARACHEK

I missed a bus once, and I was lucky. I wanted to see
if I could be lucky twice.

We are now passing a sign saying, "You Are Now Leaving Iverstown: America's Fastest Growing Industrial City."

SAM is driving his convertible, and TONI is in the passenger's seat. She looks back at the sign.

SAM MASTERSON

Don't look back baby, don't ever look back. You know
what happened to Lot's wife, don't you?

TONI MARACHEK

Whose wife?

SAM MASTERSON

Sam's wife.

TONI MARACHEK

Sam's wife.

THE END

ABOUT THE FILM

Film noir is a genre that reached its peak in the 1940s and 1950s. Characterized by dark lighting and inspired by crime fiction, it often features characters such as a tough-guy hero, mysterious beauties who may or may not be on the level, and prominent people with crimes to hide.

The Strange Love of Martha Ivers (1946) is a beloved film noir classic.

Itinerant gambler and war hero Sam Masterson (played by Van Heflin) comes back to his hometown after seventeen years, restarting a drama that left off when he ran away to the circus as a boy.

Sam encounters old acquaintances: Martha Ivers (played by Barbara Stanwyck), then a rebellious girl, now a beautiful and formidable businesswoman, and her husband, Walter O'Neil (Kirk Douglas, in an early role), a hard-drinking district attorney tormented by shadows from his past.

Sam also meets Toni Marachek (Lizabeth Scott), a deep-voiced beauty just paroled from prison, whom he rescues and befriends.

Sam's encounters with Martha, Toni, and Walter start a game in which characters vie to assess and manipulate one another's motives. The film unravels a series of events that dredge up unwholesome secrets from the past and plunge the characters into a passionate melodrama with a bloody ending.

Sam struggles between his newfound attraction to Toni, whom he alternately trusts and distrusts, and his childhood love for Martha, who almost ran away with him when they were young.

Martha Ivers also displays other traits from the film noir genre: settings perfumed with whiskey and cigarette smoke; a tension between cynicism and decency; threats of blackmail; and a tight, well-constructed plot that hinges on its characters' strengths and weaknesses.

The Rotten Tomatoes film review site rates *Martha Ivers* at 100 percent on its Tomatometer. Comments by reviewers: "a gripping film noir, all the more effective for being staged . . . as a steamy romantic melodrama"; "a brilliant film noir with fantastic performances"; "films don't get much better." *The Strange Love of Martha Ivers* will enthrall longtime fans of film noir as well as newcomers to the genre.